FAN SERVICE

JC ANDERSON

MARLEE EARL

SILVERSTONE BOOKS

Fan Service

By J.C. Anderson & Marlee Earl

ISBN-13: 978-1-967473-19-9

CHAPTER 1
LOGAN

I'M TOO DAMN TIRED FOR THIS.

It's been over twenty-four hours since I've had a real bed, and I can feel it settling into my bones. The flight back to the States is still a couple of hours away, and all I want to do is zone out—maybe close my eyes for a bit.

Instead, I've got David Park elbowing me in the ribs.

"Dude. Look at that."

I grunt. "Look at what?"

He tilts his head toward a small group of women a few rows away, speaking rapid-fire in a language I vaguely recognize… Korean, maybe?

My grandfather had fought in the Korean War and actually spoke some.

The women keep talking. Definitely Korean.

They're animated, chatting among themselves. There are four of them—one with a mask, the others without. That's when I notice it.

They aren't just attractive.

They're ridiculous.

The kind of ridiculousness that doesn't happen in real life —perfect skin, perfect hair, all of them moving in this polished, synchronized way, like they're used to cameras tracking their every step.

"Wow," is all I can say.

David exhales. "Those are easily the most attractive women I've ever seen—well, that weren't in a porno."

"Dude." I glare at him. "Read the room."

David shakes his head, ignoring me. "Definitely Korean. If that's what women look like over there, I need to reevaluate some life choices."

I smirk. "Pretty sure it's not all of them."

The group keeps chatting among themselves, completely unaware of the effect they're having on everyone around them. Then, after a few minutes, they start moving.

All except one.

She lingers. Watches them leave.

Then—without hesitation—she plops down right next to me.

And unlike the others, she's wearing a mask.

I don't say anything at first. Just glance at her from the corner of my eye.

She's close—closer than a stranger should sit when there are empty seats everywhere. The mask covers the lower half of her face, sleek and black, like something straight out of a cyberpunk movie.

Her eyes catch me as they flicker toward my hands of all

places. Like she's super interested in what I'm holding, which is a magazine. Did she want the magazine?

I make eye contact with her and then forget about whatever she was looking at. Her eyes. They're unbelievable; the most delicate blue-gray color. Wow.

David noticed too. I heard his breath hitch before he leaned in slightly. "Why's she wearing a mask? The others aren't."

Good question.

She looked at us but didn't acknowledge us, didn't say anything. Just crosses her legs and stares straight ahead, like she's waiting for something.

I can feel David vibrating with curiosity. "Dude, say something."

I was about to, the words on the tip of my tongue, but then she glanced at her phone and just as suddenly as she sat down, she stood and walked away.

David watches her go, then turns to me, eyes wide. "What the hell was that?"

I shrugged. "No idea."

"Excuse me."

Both David and I looked up to see what appears to be a *TransAir* employee.

I spook first. "Hi, can I help you?"

"Hello, gentlemen," the woman says with a dazzling smile. "It's your lucky day!"

In an absolute stroke of luck, David and I both get upgraded. First-class flights, free booze on the plane, and access to the fancy First-Class Lounge.

Which is exactly where we head as soon as the pretty TransAir employee finishes talking to us.

David keeps looking around. "I don't know what kind of glitch in the system happened, but this is awesome."

He gestures around at the high-end decor, the plush seating, the businessmen drinking whiskey like they own oil fields.

The damn place even has an ice cream bar.

Ice cream bar. It's amazing how the other side lives.

"I'm pretty sure this is the nicest place I've ever been," he continues. "Look at this—free drinks, actual food, no screaming kids... Man, the Corps did not prepare me for this level of civilization. Remind me to be a rich man."

I snort. "An idiot like you? Good luck with that."

David gives me a pained look. "That really hurts, Logan. Has anyone ever told you that you're extremely hurtful?"

I roll my eyes.

"I think I need a glass of bourbon to ease my pain."

I cock an eyebrow. "Bourbon, right. You're getting a daiquiri."

He flips me off as he gets up.

I stretch my legs out. "Just don't embarrass us."

"Who, me?" He scoffs. "I am the picture of refinement."

That's when I see her again.

Same girl. Same mask.

She's sitting near the floor-to-ceiling windows, her posture relaxed but distant, like she's here but not really. Unlike the others from her group, who are laughing and taking selfies across the room, she's completely still.

David follows my gaze. "Wait. That's—"

"Yup."

He lets out a low whistle. "Okay, so this is weird, right? First, she sits next to you for no reason, strategically close. She must want to talk to us."

I roll my eyes. "I'm pretty sure she was in here first, Captain Obvious."

David once again ignores me. "Go talk to her."

I shake my head. "And why would I do that?"

"She's hot. And I'm too shy. Get her number for me."

I throw my book at him.

David walks off laughing.

I shift my attention back to the group of girls—just as a group of guys steps forward.

"Hey, you're like, really pretty. My friends and I are going to Greece. Where's your friend—"

The girls start talking in rapid Korean amongst themselves. There's a flurry of hands and gestures, and then one of them says in very broken English:

"Uh… so… sorry. No speak English."

Then they turn back to each other, continuing their conversation.

I watch as the guys try again but eventually give up.

My phone buzzes.

> Cindy: _Sorry I missed your call. I was
> busy. Was it important?_

I let out a sigh. I try not to think about Cindy and don't reply.

I move slowly to grab my book. But when I look back to where it was—

The girl in the mask already has it.

She walks over and sits down next to me.

Then she takes off her mask.

Damn.

CHAPTER 2
LOGAN

MY BRAIN WENT BLANK.

Like I'd just taken a hit straight to the head.

This was, single-handedly, the most attractive woman I had ever seen.

And I've been to a lot of places.

I didn't react at first. I couldn't.

Her eyes—ball sack. They were sharp, alive, playful, and a grayish-blue color. Wow. Just wow. The kind of eyes that could probably get a man to do just about anything.

Then, out of nowhere, she started talking.

Fast. Bright. Completely in Korean.

I stared at her, my brain short-circuiting.

She gestured at my magazine, her voice lilting upward at the end, like she was asking me something.

I caught exactly zero percent of what she just said.

"…What?"

She paused, looked confused, then tilted her head like she was considering something, then—

She grinned.

And that's when I knew I was in serious trouble.

Because that grin—it was mischief, challenge, and confidence all wrapped up in one.

She leaned back into her seat, still watching me, still smiling, like she was perfectly content to sit here and let me figure out what the hell just happened.

And I didn't know why, but something about that made my exhaustion disappear.

Her freaking legs were unbelievably distracting; she was wearing short shorts with fuzzy boots. Her legs were long, shapely, and flawless. I tried REALLY hard not to look at them.

I cleared my throat, giving her a slow once-over.

"I saw earlier when those guys tried to talk to you. No English, huh?"

No response.

Just that smile.

"Well, I can't hold that against you. I don't speak Korean. Wish I did, though." I leaned back, stretching my legs out. "Probably would've been the highlight of my year. And trust me—it's been a pretty shitty year. Actually, it's stupid. We don't really learn languages like most countries. Hell, I barely speak English."

She just took a sip from her water bottle, eyes still locked on me.

Unreal.

Her eyes didn't indicate that she understood what I was saying, but for some reason, she seemed to be enjoying me talking at her.

And because I was too exhausted to have a filter, my mouth just… kept going.

I exhaled, shaking my head. "Since it's just you and me here, I have to ask—Not all Korean girls are in your orbit, right? Like, there are normal-looking ones too? Because this is ridiculous."

Nothing.

Just a slow blink.

"I thought people like you only existed on the Internet."

Still nothing.

I gestured vaguely at her. "I'm sure you hear it all the time. Or maybe you don't—I've heard Korean guys can be shy. Well, I don't have that problem. I'm relatively blunt. Probably the reason I didn't have many relationships before my deployment."

She tilted her head. Then said something in Korean.

I leaned forward slightly. "You know, Korean is really pretty. And your eyes are unbelievable. I am having a hard time looking at you."

She blinked once.

I sighed. What's with this sudden need to flirt with this girl?

I didn't even know her name.

"It's kind of amazing, isn't it?" I murmured. "Meeting like this, in the middle of nowhere. You—from the other side of the world. Me—just passing through."

She grinned again.

I narrowed my eyes slightly.

"You have to be someone important. Or at least on your way there."

Her eyes flickered with something—curiosity? Amusement? Hard to tell.

I tilted my head slightly. "I mean, come on. I don't know a damn thing about your personality except maybe you are full of confidence. But I'd be willing to bet my admittedly modest salary that people bend over backward for you. Strangers, friends, politicians, the Pope—probably even people who should know better."

She took another sip of her water.

I smirked slightly. "If I had to guess, you don't even ask for it. It just happens."

She adjusted her legs, stretching them. A bit of her shirt lifted, and I caught a glimpse of a flat stomach and perfect skin.

I exhaled, shaking my head. "You know, you're almost too pretty. The kind of pretty that messes with people. I bet you get hit on constantly. Maybe even by guys who should have a shot."

I paused, studying her.

"But I'd also bet that doesn't mean much. Because I think —" my voice dropped slightly, "—you feel alone anyway and most likely taken advantage of."

She looked away.

I smiled. "You don't have to worry. I have a younger sister who's a model and really cute. I know what attractive people go through. You won't have to worry about me hitting on you —even if you could understand me. You're way out of my league. So hopefully, you can feel my sincerity even if you don't understand."

The hot Korean girl's smile faltered.

She looked away, staring at her feet for a second.

And suddenly, the mood shifted. Like what I said upset her…

I cleared my throat, feeling like I'd stepped on a landmine I didn't know was there.

Before I could fix it, I heard the clatter of a cup hitting the table.

David.

He dropped into the seat across from me, holding a drink in one hand and a magazine in the other.

And then he froze.

I barely had time to react before he went completely still, eyes locked on the woman sitting next to me.

Then, like a man realizing he just walked into a minefield, he straightened up, gripping his cup like he suddenly didn't know what to do with his hands.

I laughed. "Hey, dude, I thought you were going to get me a coffee. Don't worry about her. She doesn't speak English. Super pretty though, right? Don't make it weird and make her uncomfortable."

David just stared at the girl, who gave him a big, dazzling smile.

I frowned. "What's up with you?"

David didn't answer right away. He glanced at me, then

back at her, then at me again, and his jaw actually dropped slightly.

Then, in slow motion, like he was checking to make sure he wasn't crazy, he lowered the magazine in his hand.

And right there, staring back at me—

Was her.

On the cover.

Looking stupidly perfect, wearing some designer outfit, gazing at the camera like she owned the world.

JI-AN, LEADER OF NOVA, THE K-POP GROUP TAKING THE WORLD BY STORM!

Underneath, a headline:

"Ji-an Opens Up About Her Life Between Two Worlds— Growing Up in Australia & Finding Her Place in Korea!"

My brain broke.

I stared at the magazine.

Then at her.

Then back at the magazine.

Then at David.

He looked like he was physically restraining himself from losing his mind.

"Oh my giddy aunt," he finally wheezed. "This is awesome."

I shook my head, still trying to process. "What?"

David leaned forward like he needed to make sure I understood how insane this was. "Do you have any idea who this is?"

I opened my mouth. Closed it. Slowly turned my head toward her.

Of course, I know who it is. NOW.

She was still watching me. Still grinning like a wolf.

Like she had been waiting for this moment.

David, meanwhile, was losing it.

"Bro. BRO. You just spent the last twenty minutes hitting on one of the most famous women in the world."

I dragged a hand down my face. "I wasn't hitting on her. I was just talking—."

I stopped and looked at her.

I had pretty much spent the last half hour telling her how attractive she was.

I looked back at the cover, staring at one word in particular.

Australia.

"Shit," I said.

And then she spoke.

Soft. Amused. Just loud enough for me to hear and with the slight hint of an accent.

"You should go to Korea sometime. And I think your eyes are really pretty too."

Then, smooth as silk, she stood, adjusted her bag, and walked away, her ass swaying like a freaking boat.

I watched her disappear into the crowd, my mind still trying to catch up.

David wiped tears from his eyes. "Dude. I need you to know this is the funniest thing that has ever happened."

I punched David on the arm.

CHAPTER 3

JI-AN

I FELT HIS EYES ON ME AS I DISAPPEARED INTO THE CROWD.

I tried not to look back at him. I really did.

I failed.

Our eyes met—just briefly—and he looked at me in disbelief.

I made mental notes. American. Marine. Oblivious. Handsome. His name… his name was Logan...Carter? His friend mentioned it.

I hadn't meant to sit next to him, let alone let the conversation drag out as long as it had.

Though *conversation* is a bit of a stretch. He talked. I listened.

Still, something about him—the way he carried himself, the way he talked to me like I was just some random woman in an airport—had kept me there.

And now?

Now he knew exactly who I was.

I could still hear his stunned *"shit"* ringing in my ears.

It made me smile.

Ahead of me, my group was watching me approach, clearly waiting. As soon as I reached them, Hye-won, always the most excitable, practically bounced over, her eyes flicking past me to where I'd just been.

"Unnie, who was that?"

I sighed, brushing a loose strand of hair behind my ear. "Just some American."

Jisoo snorted. "Some ridiculously hot American. Are his eyes as blue as they look from here?"

I waved her off, but I didn't deny it.

Because yeah—he *was* hot. In a very annoying, completely unfair, rugged, broad-shouldered, military-trained kind of way.

He said I was made in a lab. Has *he* looked in a mirror??

Hye-won was practically buzzing with curiosity. "Why were you talking to him? Did he recognize you?"

"No," I said smoothly, adjusting my bag. "He had no idea who I was."

Jisoo looked offended on my behalf. "How?"

I shrugged. "Not everyone watches K-pop."

Min-ji, our main dancer and the youngest among all of us, gave me a knowing look. "You looked like you were having fun."

I didn't answer right away.

Because... well.

I *had* been.

But why?

I had no business sitting next to a stranger and letting him talk to me like that. Not in a bad way—he had been borderline shameless, but there had been nothing creepy about it.

If anything, he had been too honest.

Too direct.

And somehow, too accurate.

You feel alone anyway.

I hadn't expected that.

I had thought I would throw him off with my silence. Let him spiral a little, then leave. But instead, he had read me.

And I had let him.

Min-ji was still watching me.

I needed a cover story before they started assuming things.

I took a slow breath, choosing my words carefully. "Honestly? I was just going to ask if I could look at his magazine when he was done with it."

Hye-won tilted her head. "His magazine?"

"Yeah." I waved a hand, trying to sound casual. "I was waiting for him to put it down, but then I accidentally asked in Korean and, well..." I sighed dramatically. "He was cute, so I just let him talk."

Jisoo snorted. "He was cute, so you let him talk? That's cold."

I smirked. "Yeah. A bit."

Min-ji eyed me suspiciously. "What magazine?"

I hesitated.

And this was where I needed to be careful.

Because the real answer?

A gun magazine.

And no matter how much I tried to convince myself otherwise, idols weren't supposed to be into guns.

Not publicly.

Not in interviews.

And definitely not in an international airport where anyone could see me drooling over the specs of the new KS-90 Rail Rifle—an absolute beast of a weapon with next-gen recoil compensation, custom porting, and a hybrid thermal-optic scope.

I bit my lip.

I wanted to see that article.

Badly.

But I could already imagine the scandal that would follow.

"Jia of NOVA is secretly obsessed with deadly firearms?!"

Yeah. No thanks.

I needed a different answer.

"…It was a travel magazine," I lied smoothly. "There was an article about Australia. You know, childhood nostalgia and all that."

Min-ji narrowed her eyes. "Mmmhmm."

I shot her my most innocent look. "What?"

She held up her hands in surrender. "Nothing. Just… it's been a long time since I've seen you voluntarily start a conversation with a guy."

I scoffed. "Conversation is probably a stretch. I sat down,

said the wrong thing, and then he just... kept talking. I did answer him in Korean a couple of times."

Jisoo shook her head, still looking amused. "So you let a hot American flirt with you for twenty minutes because you were too embarrassed to ask for a magazine?"

"...Yes."

Hye-won grinned. "I kind of love that. Our *Unnie* has grown up!"

Min-ji was still looking at me. Not in a judgmental way— just *thoughtful*.

I ignored it.

"Anyway," I said briskly. "It's not like it matters. He knows who I am now. So it's over."

Jisoo chuckled. "He looked like his soul left his body when his friend showed him that magazine."

I smirked. "Yeah. That was fun."

Hye-won sighed dramatically. "I wish I had that kind of luck. Attractive men never randomly flirt with me in airports."

"Maybe because you don't give them a chance," Min-ji pointed out. "You always have your headphones in."

Hye-won gasped. "Excuse me, music is my priority!"

Jisoo laughed, linking arms with her. "Come on, let's get to our gate before we miss this flight."

We started walking again, but I didn't immediately follow.

I glanced back toward the waiting area—just for a second.

Logan was still sitting there, staring at the magazine like he was trying to process his entire life.

David, meanwhile, looked like he was in actual pain from laughing so hard.

I smirked.

Then turned and walked away.

I didn't know if I'd ever see Logan Carter again.

But I kind of hoped I would. I felt his eyes on me as I disappeared into the crowd.

CHAPTER 4
LOGAN

I'D BEEN BACK FOR THREE MONTHS.

Three months of trying to figure out what the hell to do next. Three months of readjusting to civilian life, dodging questions from old neighbors, and pretending like I gave a damn about small talk.

Three months of Cindy not letting it go. Man… do I wish she would let go.

I wasn't mad anymore. Not really. Not sure I ever really was.

Finding out she'd been cheating had sucked, but it hadn't destroyed me or anything. I had been with Cindy off and on for like five years, and before I left on my first deployment, she wanted a stronger commitment, so I was like, fine.

Apparently, that desire for commitment—at least for me—didn't last that long.

Like I said, though, ultimately, it's not that big of a deal. It wasn't like we were engaged or anything. I am a little baffled at how I didn't see it coming. I came to the conclusion that I sort of knew and just didn't care enough to address it. But by the time I walked in and saw her curled up with Derrick Owens like he was the love of her life, I felt more annoyed than anything because honestly, I like that couch.

Cindy's cheating was part of the reason I didn't sign the lease at the beginning of this year. Even back then, I think I had an inkling.

I walked into the apartment that day. "Hey, Derrick. Hey, Cindy."

They both panicked.

"Logan," Cindy said. "This isn't what it looks like. Let me explain—"

I simply put a hand up. "It's okay, Cindy. We all know exactly what it looks like. Just let me grab my stuff, and I'll be out of your hair."

I grabbed a duffel, threw in some clothes and other items, and left with my sister, Emily.

Honestly, I'm not sure what they were expecting. Maybe they wanted the drama of a scene—a fight, maybe even an arrest. But I guess I just didn't care that much.

Strange, I know.

So now, it's three months later, and I'm trying to move on.

Cindy, though? She wanted… well, I'm not sure what she wanted. I think she wanted me to be upset. She wanted me to see her with Derrick.

I don't know if she thought I'd be heartbroken by her actions or if she was surprised at the fact that I really wasn't that broken up about her. Honestly, I'm not sure how I feel. But I'm not going to get all bent out of shape about it.

What I don't understand is her behavior since that night I came home. Maybe she just liked the idea of me watching her play house with Derrick, but whatever the reason, she made sure she was everywhere I was.

The coffee shop. The grocery store. The gym.

If I was there, she'd show up within the hour, hanging all over Derrick like they were in some low-budget romance movie.

It was really annoying.

And Emily was ready to kill her.

The second my sister walked into the bar and saw me, she was already scowling.

"I swear to Aisha, Logan, if I see her one more time acting the vapid shank, I'm going to beat the hell out of her."

I sighed, taking a slow sip of my whiskey. "Nice to see you too, Em."

"I mean it." She dropped her purse onto the bar and slid onto the stool next to me, crossing her arms like she'd been preparing this rant all day. "The way she acts with Derrick?? Can someone tell me when we got transported to a teen drama from the '90s? I would love to know. And how does she do this to my loving older brother? Who does she think she is? She shall not get away with this! I will have my revenge."

Besides modeling, did I mention my sister is a drama major? I'm sure you're shocked by that one.

"Emily."

"No, because seriously! Who does that? Who spends years with someone and then parades their new boyfriend around like they need a damn trophy?"

I shook my head, but I couldn't help the small smirk forming. Emily takes my breakups way too personally if you haven't noticed. She often gets more upset than I do.

"Cindy… is looking for something," I said simply. "She thinks attention, or validation, or whatever is going to help her find it. I'm pretty sure me not reacting the way she thought I would is driving her crazy. She thinks she'll find whatever it is she's looking for by making me react."

Emily leaned forward, eyes blazing. "Then why don't we give her something to react to? You know, fire with fire."

I raised an eyebrow. "Nothing you just said made any sense. And what exactly does that mean?"

She grinned. "You need a date."

I groaned and took another sip of whiskey. "No."

"Yes."

"No."

"Logan."

I exhaled. "Emily."

She rolled her eyes. "Listen, I'm not saying fall in love. I'm saying go out, have fun, dance, or fish, or get laid—do something. Remind everyone in this town that Cindy wasn't the best thing to ever happen to you."

I shook my head. "I don't need to prove anything to Cindy."

Emily stared at me for a long moment, then grabbed her phone and started scrolling.

I frowned. "What are you doing?"

"Looking up single women in Ellensburg."

I groaned. "Emily—"

"Would you rather I check Yakima? What about MoTown? Oh! You could take a girl out on the lake!" She flicked through her contacts. "I have a friend who works at Samaritan Hospital. She says the new nurses are cute."

I shook my head, laughing under my breath. "I don't need a damn setup."

She leaned on the bar, grinning. "Then do it yourself."

I rolled my eyes, but for the first time in weeks, I felt a little lighter.

Emily nudged my arm. "Come on. One date. What's the worst that could happen?"

I glanced down at my glass, turning it in my hands.

She wasn't wrong.

And honestly?

Maybe it's time.

"Okay. I'll think about it."

Emily's face lit up like a Christmas tree. She smiled, then grimaced like she'd just remembered something. "Oh, I have a message for you. It's that facilities guy from the corporation that bought the Gorge."

I nodded. "Mr. Otto? I wonder why he's reaching out."

Emily shrugged. "Hopefully to give you a job."

I snorted. One could only hope.

CHAPTER 5
JI-AN

THE CROWD IS STILL SCREAMING.

Even from backstage, I can hear them—tens of thousands of fans chanting our names, the energy in the arena still electric even though the show ended twenty minutes ago.

I should be buzzing too. Should be running on that post-performance high, giddy with adrenaline.

Instead, I'm scrolling through my phone, half-listening as the rest of the girls take turns collapsing into the dressing room chairs.

"You killed it out there, Ji-an."

Hye-won and Jisoo flop down next to me, still breathless from the encore.

I hum in agreement, not really paying attention.

The show had been good. Great, even. But my brain isn't on the performance.

It's the picture glowing softly on my screen of a man who wasn't my boyfriend.

He sat alone at the bar, one arm resting casually on the counter, the other cradling a glass of whiskey like it was the only thing keeping him tethered to the moment. His frame was powerful, not oversized, but compact—all clean lines and coiled strength, like someone carved out of tension and discipline.

One might think he was a cop with the automatic sitting in a holster on the bar. But he wasn't.

His jaw was set, his expression unreadable—the kind of face that made strangers think twice about starting a conversation. His sleeves were rolled to the elbows, forearms marked with the subtle definition of someone who didn't need a gym to be dangerous.

Logan Carter.

He didn't smile in the photo. Of course he didn't.

He never smiled for cameras.

And yet, something about the image…

Made it feel like he was looking straight through the lens—right at me.

I don't know why I looked him up. I told myself it was curiosity at first. A harmless, fleeting thought that had turned into a quick search. But now, three months later, I still find myself doing it more often than I'd like to admit.

It's not weird. I am just a girl who was curious about a boy. Simple.

I doubt he even remembers me. It's a bit of a secret because sometimes, when things slow down—between rehearsals, on flights, in quiet hotel rooms—I think about the way he looked at me before he knew who I was.

Like I was just a normal person. Like I wasn't Ji-an of NOVA—K-pop's golden girl, the face on every billboard from Seoul to LA—but just some random woman in an airport who sat next to him and let him ramble himself into a hole.

That night had stuck with me in a way I hadn't expected.

And now here I am, three months later, lying in bed, staring at pictures of him like an idiot.

It's not even his account. His is private. Of course it is.

This one's his sister's—Emily.

Yes, I figured out he has a sister named Emily.

Yes, she's a model.

Yes, she's super pretty.

No, I'm not insecure.

Okay, maybe a little.

But that's not the point.

The point is: he's in the background of one of her stories.

Logan.

Leaning against the edge of a shooting bay at some tactical range in Arizona, wearing a ball cap, black tee, and that same "don't talk to me unless you're bleeding or on fire" expression.

And in his hands? A custom Nighthawk TRS Comp—one of the sexiest pieces of American engineering I'd ever seen.

Yes, I looked it up.

Yes, I know exactly what that is now.

Don't judge me.

The gun was matte black with a built-in compensator and optic-ready slide—basically something that looked like it could punch holes in goddamn reality.

And he held it like it was just another part of his body.

Comfortable. Efficient. Dangerous.

Just like him.

I zoomed in, paused the screen.

And for half a second, he glanced toward the camera.

Not quite smiling.

But not not-smiling either.

Like he knew.

Like he always knew.

I sigh, rubbing my temples. I should be worrying about the actual scandal circling my name right now, not reminiscing about some random Marine I met once and lusting after his sidearm.

(If you're wondering about what scandal, I had been recently connected, somehow, to some up-and-coming Chinese actor who apparently has a crush on me. It was all the talk right now. He has been trying to set coffee with my agency.)

"You look way too serious for someone who just finished an amazing show."

Min-ji's voice breaks through my thoughts.

I blink and glance up.

She's standing a few feet away, still holding a water bottle, eyes flicking between me and my phone screen.

She is suspicious.

Shit.

I casually tilt my phone away from her line of sight. "I'm just tired."

Her eyes narrow.

Double shit.

Min-ji doesn't move.

Neither do her eyebrows, which are definitely raised in a 'yeah, sure' kind of way.

In case you were wondering, Min-ji is the smartest among us. She is close to a freaking genius. Or so she says.

"Uh-huh." She takes a slow sip of water. "And does being tired usually involve staring at pictures of extremely attractive men?"

Triple shit, shit, shit, shit.

I do not react.

At least, I try not to.

Unfortunately, Hye-won's ears perk up at the word "attractive men."

"Wait, what? Who?"

Before I can stop her, Min-ji lunges.

I yank my phone away, but it's too late.

Hye-won, Min-ji, and now Jisoo are all gathered around me, peering over my shoulder.

There is no escape.

And then it happens.

The collective gasp.

The moment where they see what I've been looking at.

Min-ji narrows her eyes. "Wait a second. He looks familiar."

Jisoo tilts her head. "Oh my Lordy. Is that—"

"No one." I lock my phone and shove it into my pocket before they can start forming actual theories. "It's literally no one. Don't be weird."

Hye-won isn't buying it. She's looking at me with a look.

The kind of look that says, *I know exactly what this is, and I'm about to be unbearable about it.*

I shoot her a warning glance. "Don't."

She grins. "I mean, I just think it's interesting. You, looking up pictures of a—"

"Don't."

"A certain handsome American Marine you met in an airport—"

I groan. "Hye-won."

"—who, by the way, I remember you flirting with."

"I did not flirt."

Min-ji laughs. "You let him talk himself into a meltdown while you sat there and smirked. That's your version of flirting."

I glare. "Why do I even talk to you people?"

Jisoo walks over to the couch, plops down, and stretches her arms. "I don't know, but I'm fascinated. I thought you weren't interested in dating for a while?"

"I'm not."

Min-ji raises a brow. "Then why are you stalking a random guy from three months ago?"

I throw my hands in the air. "I'm not stalking him! I was just—he came up in my feed, and I clicked on it. That's it."

Hye-won clutches her chest. "You follow him?"

"No, of course not. Can you imagine what would happen if I did?"

"But you searched for him," Jisoo points out, eyes twinkling with amusement.

I pinch the bridge of my nose. "You're all the worst."

Min-ji shrugs. "We're not saying you like him."

"Good."

"But if you did," she continues, ignoring me, "it would be kind of adorable."

I groan dramatically, slumping back into the chair. "You bitches sure are bold today."

They're never going to let this go.

Not now.

Not when I've been in the headlines all week over the breakup that wasn't even a real breakup.

They don't say it, but I know what they're thinking. That this is convenient timing.

I'm looking up Logan Carter because I need a distraction.

And maybe I am.

But that doesn't mean anything.

Right?

CHAPTER 6
LOGAN

ANOTHER NINE MONTHS PASS.

Another change of plans.

If you told me a year ago I'd be working security for one of the biggest music venues in the Pacific Northwest, I'd have laughed in your face.

Hell, even six months ago, I didn't expect to be here.

But when I got home, I needed a job and started working security, having had some prior experience before my development. It was a good job, paid well, but not something I could do full-time.

Then, when spring concert season rolled around, the Gorge asked me to come back. They were looking for someone with my background—military experience, logistics, crowd control. They had taken advantage of these traits of mine last year.

I had no expectations for this year.

At first, I figured it was temporary. A side gig while I

figured out my next move. But then the venue kept calling me back, throwing more money at me, asking for input on operations. Before I knew it, I wasn't just working security—I was running it.

There was a fallout with their security company's president.

Then they wanted me to start a company and bid for the Gorge security contract.

Me? A business owner?

Sounds insane.

But the money's there. So after some scrambling, I put together a security company. I secured funding from a rich uncle, hired guys—mostly locals with a military background —set up training, and now we have a company.

I'm even getting offers to head up security for other places in Seattle and as far away as San Francisco. But I couldn't leave the Gorge. I love this place.

People who've never been don't get it. The way the sun sets behind the stage, painting the Columbia River gold. The way the amphitheater sits on the edge of the cliffs, how the grass replaces traditional seating, making every concert feel like something bigger than just a show.

The venue hasn't changed much in the last thirty years.

The music industry? Different story.

Back in high school, I saw a Summer Jam here—Eminem, Dr. Dre, Busta Rhymes, even Beyoncé. Big names. Legends.

Now? The biggest show in years isn't some rock band or a hip-hop festival.

It's a K-pop group.

Nova.

I swear to everything holy, the world has lost its damn mind.

I don't get it. K-pop isn't just popular—it's religion-level hysteria. These fans treat groups like Nova like they're the second coming of Jesus, and security has been tripled just to handle them.

Which is why I'm here.

I'm making more money in one night than I made in almost my entire time in the Marines.

Yeah, that's a big-ass number.

But the chaos hasn't fully hit yet. The show's tomorrow, fans are just starting to arrive, and we've got time to breathe.

Which is why the team decided to grab food at a small diner about thirty miles away in Moses Lake before the real madness starts.

The place is nothing special. An old-school, family-owned joint with a faded menu and booths that have seen better days.

Perfect for a quiet meal.

Or at least, it should be.

I'm halfway through my steak when the diner door swings open.

And I hear it before I see it.

That laugh.

Loud. Annoying.

Cindy.

And, of course, she's not alone.

Derrick Owens, smug as ever, strolls in beside her, his hand resting possessively on her waist.

I don't react.

Don't care enough to.

I just keep eating, barely acknowledging them.

But Cindy?

Cindy isn't going to let that happen.

She wants a reaction. I can see it in the set of her jaw, in the way she's talking just a little too loudly.

What the hell is wrong with her?

I can feel my coworkers watching, most of them local guys who know the history. But they also know my complete indifference.

I cut another piece of steak. Take a sip of my drink. Let them squirm in their own desperation.

Cindy cracks first.

She saunters closer, her voice syrupy sweet. "Wow, Logan. Didn't think I'd see you here."

I don't even bother looking up. "Sure, Cindy. I'm sure you had no idea."

Her smile falters. Not what she expected.

Derrick, always eager to be the biggest asshole in the room, steps in.

"Didn't know you were still around. Thought you'd be somewhere... I don't know, being poor."

I snort. "Ahh, yes. The classic 'you're poor' insult. Real creative, Derrick." I glance at him, unimpressed. "The 1980s called, and they want their dialogue back. Besides, I'd rather be poor than have a silver spoon up my ass."

A couple of the guys at my table choke back laughter.

Derrick's jaw tightens, but he keeps talking.

"You seem tense, Logan. Maybe you should take a vacation." He smirks, pulling Cindy closer like she's a prize. "Actually, Cindy and I just got back from California. First class. Saw the Redwoods. Maybe I should send you our travel agent's number."

I hum, unimpressed. "Good for you. How'd all that go with the OARC complaints you've been getting?"

Derrick freezes.

Like a deer in freaking headlights. "You know about that?"

I grin. "Everyone knows about that. That's what happens when you use ChatGPT to write your legal briefs, dumbass."

The guys at my table lose it.

Derrick's face darkens. Cindy shifts uncomfortably.

She tries to recover. "Logan, I didn't realize you were so petty. I'm disappointed."

I raise an eyebrow. "You did just hear him make fun of me for being poor, right? Maybe you should worry less about me and more about your boyfriend, who's about to lose his law license."

I take a slow sip of my drink, watching as her confidence crumbles.

Derrick, realizing Cindy is completely failing, tries one last jab.

"I will be fine, Logan. Don't worry about me and mine. You just keep doing your little security job. Isn't that a bit pathetic? Weren't you, like, valedictorian at one point? What happened to being smart?"

I smirk. "I don't know. Protecting people from entitled assholes like you seems like the *smart* thing to do."

The table erupts into laughter.

Derrick's face reddens.

Cindy looks like she swallowed a lemon.

I level a look at Derrick. "Blow it out your ass, Derrick, and take your, uh, girlfriend with you."

CHAPTER 7
JI-AN

I SHOULD BE ASLEEP.

The show is tomorrow, and I need to be rested, but instead, I'm lying in bed, wrapped up in a hotel robe, scrolling through my secret account with the dim glow of my phone lighting up the dark room.

I tell myself I'm just checking messages. That's it.

But then I see it.

A video.

I pause.

The thumbnail is blurry, just a shot of some nondescript diner, but the caption catches my eye.

"Ex-Marine shuts down ex and her new boyfriend without even trying."

Something about it makes me click.

At first, I don't recognize the setting. Just another small-town American restaurant, the kind with laminated menus and waitresses who call you "hon." But then the camera shifts, and my stomach flips.

Logan.

He's sitting at a table, looking completely at ease, while a blonde woman stands across from him, her arms folded, her expression way too pleased with herself.

Cindy.

I narrow my eyes.

"So we meet again."

When I first found Logan's social media, I did a bit of digging. Not in a stalkery way—I was just curious about his life. I found his sister's social media. She's a big K-pop fan, by the way, and she had posted about Cindy cheating on Logan.

The bitch.

Who cheats on a guy when he's fighting for lives on the other side of the world?

She had been with her new boyfriend for over a year now.

Cindy is smiling in the video. She's pretty enough, I guess, in a generic, over-processed kind of way. Blonde, blue-eyed, perfectly made-up—the type that probably spends an hour on her hair just to make it look "effortless."

But still.

Not pretty enough for him.

Not by a long shot.

I press play.

The first thing I hear is her laugh.

Loud. Annoying. Fake.

I grimace and turn the volume down a little.

The camera shakes slightly as the person recording shifts.

Cindy is standing next to Logan's table, her hand resting on her hip, while some guy—her boyfriend, I'm guessing—leans in, looking just as smug.

I don't know what I expect, but Logan barely reacts. If anything, he looks somewhat amused.

He just keeps eating, like they're not even worth looking at.

Cindy, clearly not satisfied with that, leans closer. "Wow, Logan. Didn't think I'd see you here."

His response is so dry I almost laugh. "Sure, Cindy. I'm sure you had no idea."

Her smile falters for half a second.

I smirk.

Oh, this is going to be good.

The boyfriend, desperate to assert himself, jumps in. "Didn't know you were still around. Thought you'd be somewhere… I don't know, being poor."

I gasp so hard I nearly choke on my own spit.

No. He. Did. Not.

Who says that?

But Logan? He doesn't even flinch.

He just snorts. "Ahh, yes, the classic 'you're poor' insult. Real creative, Derrick. The 1980s called, and they want their dialogue back. Besides, I'd rather be poor than have a silver spoon up my ass."

I cover my mouth to keep from laughing.

Derrick—his name *had* to be Derrick. He's a dick. I can already tell.

Logan goes back to eating, completely unbothered, but

Derrick, clearly irritated that he's not getting a reaction, keeps going.

"You seem really tense, Logan. Maybe you should try going on vacation. Actually, Cindy and I just got back from California. First class. Saw the Redwoods, the works. Maybe I should send you our travel agent's number."

I roll my eyes so hard they might detach.

Good lord, I hate guys like this.

Logan doesn't even look up. "Good for you. How'd all that go with the OARC complaints you've been getting?"

The entire mood shifts.

Derrick freezes. "You know about that?"

Logan grins. "Everyone knows about that. That's what happens when you use ChatGPT to write your legal briefs, dumbass."

I choke out a laugh.

The guys at Logan's table are dying.

Derrick looks like he just swallowed his own tie. Cindy, still trying to salvage the moment, tries to switch gears.

"Logan, I didn't realize you were so petty. I'm disappointed."

Oh, this woman is desperate.

Logan just lifts an eyebrow. "You did just hear him make fun of me for being poor, right? Maybe you should worry less about me and more about your boyfriend, who's about to lose his law license."

The way Cindy visibly shrinks makes me grin.

Derrick, realizing his girlfriend is drowning, tries one last jab.

"I will be fine, Logan; don't worry about me and mine. You just keep doing your little security job. Isn't that a bit pathetic? Weren't you, like, valedictorian at one point? What happened to being smart?"

Logan smirks. "I don't know. Protecting people from entitled assholes like you seems like the smart thing to do."

The entire table erupts.

Derrick's face turns red.

Cindy looks like she's been personally offended by gravity.

And Logan?

He just stands up, tosses some money onto the table, and walks out like it's just another day.

The video ends.

I stare at my screen for a long moment, then go straight to the comments section.

"Dude didn't even blink. King behavior."

"I need to know everything about this man immediately."

"The way he just ate his steak while they embarrassed themselves... I need this energy in my life."

"I've never seen someone be so attractive while doing so little."

"What's OARC?"

"Office of Attorney Regulation - this guy is a lawyer??? What an ass!"

I smirk, shaking my head.

Logan Carter, unknowingly entering his viral era.

I should stop watching.

I should put my phone down and go to sleep.

Instead, I click on the location tag.

And that's when it hits me.

This diner?

It's right down the street.

I sit up straighter, my heart kicking up a notch.

Of course, it makes sense—Moses Lake is the closest town to the Gorge, and Logan's working security there.

But still.

He's here.

Closer than he's ever been.

I don't know what I'm doing until my fingers are already typing.

> @Wanderlust_J: "So, you're famous now?"

I hit send before I can overthink it.

A few minutes pass.

Then—

> Logan_Carter: You saw that, did you? Dumb, right? People are too attached to their phones. Didn't realize having dinner was a viral event. And isn't it, like, super early where you are? Should you be working or something? I should get to bed. I am going to have a long day tomorrow.

I grin.

Because tomorrow?

Tomorrow, I'm finally going to see him again.

And he still has no idea.

I stare at my phone long after Logan's message disappears from the screen, my heart still hammering in my chest.

I should go to sleep.

I really should.

But my brain won't shut off.

It's been almost a year since I first stumbled across his social media.

Okay, that was a lie. I didn't stumble. I looked and found him. It actually wasn't that hard. I remembered his full name and started searching. It didn't take me long.

At the time, his profile was locked down—private, barely updated, almost like he didn't want to be found. But I was determined.

I don't even remember what made me so curious in the first place. Maybe it was how he carried himself in that short interaction we had, or the fact that he unloaded his true thoughts.

I don't know.

But after months of being unable to forget about him, I broke down and looked for him and befriended him.

And now, I'm going to see him.

I'm going to tell him who I am.

And then, I'm going to hope that when he knows...

He won't hate me.

CHAPTER 8
LOGAN

THE MORNING STARTED LIKE ANY OTHER.

I arrived at The Gorge early, radio clipped to my vest, running through the final security protocols before the madness hit. The sun was already climbing over the cliffs, casting a golden glow over the amphitheater. It was quiet now—just the crew moving equipment, vendors setting up, and the security team doing their final walkthroughs before the storm hit.

And it was going to be a storm.

Nova's show was tonight.

The crowds were already forming, with fans camping out for days, and by mid-afternoon, the lines would be spilling into the fields beyond the gates.

I had worked on plenty of big events, but nothing like this. K-pop fans weren't just fans. They were a force. A loud, dedicated, slightly unhinged force.

Ray, one of the senior security guys, fell in step beside me. "You ready for this, boss?"

I snorted. "Not even close."

He smirked. "Never thought we'd see the day. A bunch of teenage girls breaking you, Carter?"

"I'm not worried about them," I said, scanning the perimeter. "I'm worried about the psychos who think they can rush the barricades. This is the kind of crowd that'll climb a fence and throw themselves at moving vehicles to get a glimpse of their idols."

Ray nodded. "No joke. You see the numbers for this one? We've got twice the usual security detail. Even hired some guys from out of state. No risks."

"Good," I said. "I want everyone tight on protocol. Checkpoints need to be flawless. No one without clearance gets through backstage. No exceptions."

"Got it."

We walked the grounds, making rounds, checking placements, making sure every part of the amphitheater was covered. By now, I had this place memorized.

But today felt different.

It wasn't just another show.

I could feel it—an itch at the back of my mind.

Something nagging at me.

I tried to shake it off, focusing on the job. We finished the last checkpoint sweep, and I was about to head back to the operations tent when I saw it.

The posters.

Massive promotional materials being set up at the entrance.

Bright colors. Glossy finishes.

And her.

Ji-an.

I stopped mid-step, eyes locking onto the larger-than-life image of her in the center.

Her posture was fluid, confident. Long lines. Clean angles. Every part of her posed like she knew exactly what she was doing—and exactly what kind of effect it had. Her dark hair framed her face in smooth, flawless sheets, the kind of hair that made you wonder if it was real or some studio trick. Her mouth, slightly parted, gave just enough softness to balance out the cut of her jaw and cheekbones.

But it was her eyes that did it.

Focused. Direct. Like they weren't looking *at* the camera— they were looking *through* it. Through anyone watching.

Even if I hadn't already known who she was, I would have stopped. Anyone would have stopped.

But I did know who she was.

And for a second, everything else—the security checks, the job, the constant motion—just stilled.

I hadn't even let myself think about it.

I had known Nova was performing, had known this was a massive event, but I ignored the thoughts that came surrounding her.

I had met her once.

Months ago, in an airport. Before I had any clue who she was.

Before I had watched her sit down next to me, completely unreadable, and let me dig myself into a hole. Before I had ranted about how unfairly attractive she was, completely unaware that she was one of the most famous women on the planet.

The memory gave me a small kick now.

Embarrassing.

Still, I hadn't said anything untrue. She was too pretty. She did probably have the world at her feet. And if I had to bet, she was lonely, too.

I wondered if she would recognize me.

Probably not.

Why would she?

I was just some guy she had crossed paths with in an airport. Some idiot who had talked too much while she sat there, silently laughing at me.

Meanwhile, she was everywhere.

I had even looked her up after the fact. Watched a couple of interviews. Checked out some of her music—not that I would admit that to anyone.

I had hovered over the follow button on her social media more than once.

Never actually did it. Wasn't that brave yet.

Deep in thought, a message popped up.

@Wanderlust_J: Good luck today!

I smiled. Jess. It had been a bit since I heard from her.

I exhaled, shaking my head slightly.

I didn't even know how that had started.

One day, I had just gotten a message from some blonde girl from New Zealand. Big personality. Bigger opinions.

She was sharp—funnier than I expected, witty in a way that made our conversations easy. She gave me shit constantly, but not in a way that felt mean.

We talked a lot. More than I talked to most people.

I didn't have many friends—not the kind you just message in the middle of the night when you're bored or stuck on something stupid like what to eat for dinner. But somehow, Jess became that.

She called me out when I was being an idiot. She challenged me on things I hadn't even realized I had opinions about. We talked endlessly about guns, food, and travel. She was hella cool. Somewhere along the way, she started to matter.

Which was insane, because I had never even met her.

She was just some random girl I talked to online.

And yet, I trusted her.

"You good?" Ray asked, noticing my pause.

I blinked, forcing myself to move, to shrug like nothing was off. "Yeah. Just taking it in."

"Crazy, huh? Never thought I'd see the day—Logan Carter, front and center at a K-pop show."

I smirked. "Don't get used to it."

Before Ray could say anything else, the radio on my vest crackled.

"Carter, the tour's head of security just arrived. He's looking for you."

I exhaled. "On my way."

One last glance at the poster.

Then I turned and walked away.

Because tonight?

Tonight, Ji-an and the rest of Nova would be here.

And in the middle of a 100,000-person crowd, I had a weird feeling—

That something was about to change.

CHAPTER 9
JI-AN

THE TOUR BUS RUMBLED TO A STOP, THE SOFT HUM OF THE engine fading as the door swung open.

Outside, the air was dry and crisp, the silence almost unsettling after weeks of city noise—no honking cars, no neon-lit chaos, just endless hills rolling toward the river.

Moses Lake had been quaint enough—tiny by any real standard, gorgeous sunsets, and the tranquility of the lake. But The Gorge?

It was breathtaking.

The amphitheater sat on the edge of a canyon, over-looking the Columbia River, carved into the land with the precision of divine oversight. The cliffs, the endless sky, the sheer openness of it all—it was nothing like the arenas we usually played.

It felt almost too peaceful for a Nova concert.

"Wow," Min-ji murmured, pressing her forehead against the window. "I didn't think it would be this pretty."

"I did," Hye-won said, stretching. "I looked it up. This place is legendary."

Jisoo made a face. "It looks like the kind of place people go camping. Are we performing, or are we supposed to be pitching tents?"

Hye-won smirked. "You wouldn't last ten minutes outside."

I barely registered the conversation.

I wasn't listening.

I was too busy scrolling through my messages, checking for an update that wasn't there.

I had messaged Logan last night, the last thing I'd done before falling asleep.

> Wanderlust_J: So, you're famous now?

His response was casual.

> Logan_Carter: You saw that, did you? Dumb, right? People are too attached to their phones. Didn't realize having dinner was a viral event. Isn't it super early where you are? Shouldn't you be working or something? I should get to bed. I'm going to have a long day tomorrow.

And that was it.

No extra message.

No "Talk to you later."

Nothing.

Which was stupid because it wasn't like we had planned to meet up. It wasn't like Logan even knew I was secretly messaging him from a second account because I was too much of a coward to message him directly. I knew all that. But still—

I had expected something more.

Something that acknowledged the fact that I was going to be in his orbit again.

And now?

Now I was already here, stepping off the bus, the dry air hitting my skin, the venue's security team lining up near the entrance—

And then I saw him.

Way sooner than I expected.

Logan.

Walking the grounds, looking serious and contemplative. He looked bigger in person. Broad shoulders, confident stride. Tanned forearms. He looked handsome. So damn handsome even from this far away.

I froze.

My stomach did something weird, and I hated it.

I had spent weeks thinking about this moment. Imagining what it would be like to see him again.

I had pictured a lot of scenarios.

This wasn't one of them.

Because in all my overthinking, I had assumed we would meet gradually. Like I would open the door, slip on a banana peel, and fall into his arms.

Yes. I know that is ridiculous. Shut up. The point is I

wasn't expecting to see him right after I got to the freakin' venue. My heart isn't ready.

Ready or not... now he was right there, completely unaware that I was watching him.

I wanted to march over and demand his attention; tell him I missed him, that I was actually Jess and I had been thinking about him for this whole year.

Instead, I just stood there. Caught between annoyance and something dangerously close to excitement.

The others were still gathering their things, chatting with staff, completely oblivious to the fact that I had just been mentally punched in the gut.

And Logan?

Logan didn't even look in my direction.

Which was ridiculous.

I was right here.

There was no way he hadn't noticed the entire tour group pulling in. No way he hadn't clocked the arrival of one of the biggest acts in the world. No way he didn't know that the girl he talked to last year was the same one standing in front of him.

And yet—

He wasn't rushing over.

Wasn't making eye contact.

Wasn't acknowledging me at all.

He just kept walking. Focused. Professional. Talking to his security team like I wasn't even there.

My jaw tightened.

The logical part of me knew this was fine.

He was working. He wasn't some random fan at the barricades—he was security, handling a high-profile event, and he was in charge.

And I was an artist here to perform.

There was no reason for him to stop what he was doing just to talk to me. He didn't know I was Jess and that we were friends.

But that didn't mean it didn't annoy the hell out of me.

Because it did, in fact, annoy the ever-loving hell out of me.

I folded my arms, watching him move through the venue. He should know. He should know that I am here and that we have a connection.

Stupid man.

Jisoo, still standing next to me, finally noticed my mood shift.

"Uh... you good?"

I exhaled sharply, snapping myself out of it.

"Fine," I muttered, grabbing my bag and heading toward the dressing rooms.

Jisoo blinked after me. "O-kay."

I barely heard her.

My mind was already elsewhere.

Because as much as I tried to pretend otherwise, this had rattled me.

And I hated that.

I hadn't expected to feel this thrown off.

I hadn't expected to care this much.

But now, all I could think about was that the next time I saw Logan—

I wasn't going to let him walk away so easily.

CHAPTER 10
LOGAN

THE SUN WAS RELENTLESS.

High, bright, burning against the dry Washington air, casting long shadows over The Gorge.

I barely noticed.

I had too much work to do.

The venue was already alive with motion. Crew members scurried across the grounds, running cables, adjusting lighting, setting up last-minute equipment. Security teams patrolled the entry points, reinforcing barricades, double-checking wristbands and clearance lists.

Nova's fans were already gathering outside, even though the show wasn't for hours. Thousands of them. Many had been camped out since yesterday.

K-pop fans weren't just fans.

They were a movement.

I had worked high-profile events before, nothing large or grand or with people this "important." But this?

This was something else entirely.

I was scanning the perimeter, making sure the VIP pathways were clear, when one of the guys on my team—Nate, a former Army MP—sidled up next to me, a smirk on his face.

"Hey, Carter. Do you think K-pop idols have groupies? You know, those guys who follow bands and hook up with the members?"

I shot him a look. "I don't think girl groups do that sort of thing, Nate."

He grinned. "If you hear otherwise, let me know. I'd like to put in my application for groupie number one."

I rolled my eyes. "You're an idiot."

He nodded toward the entrance, where the tour buses had just pulled in and Nova had started to exit.

"Let the magic begin," he muttered. "They don't even have to try. They just step off the bus, and it's like the world tilts a little."

I raised an eyebrow at him. "Dude, that was strangely poetic."

He nodded seriously. "I'm a wordsmith. It's amazing I don't have a girlfriend."

"I'm not surprised," I said dryly. "That's what happens when you're an idiot."

"Captain. You called me an idiot twice. That really hurt."

We stopped to watch as the four members of Nova greeted fans with backstage passes and members of the press.

I studied them. Everything about them was polished. Effortless. Expensive.

Not in a forced way, either. They just existed like that.

Even in simple outfits—leggings, sneakers, oversized hoodies—they looked like they'd walked off a movie set.

Perfect posture. Perfect skin. Hair that caught the breeze like it was contractually obligated to move in slow motion.

And the way they moved?

It wasn't rehearsed. But it was practiced.

Like they'd been trained for years to step into any space and own it.

Nate leaned in again. "David told me you met Ji-an once upon a time. True story?"

I glowered at him. "David has a big mouth. Where is that jackass?"

Nate nodded behind him. "Back at the main entrance."

There was a small commotion as the Nova girls tried to get moving again. We watched Ji-an pause for a few selfies with fans.

Damn, she was cute—just as pretty as I remembered.

Jacob, one of the junior security guys, whistled softly under his breath. "This is gonna be a long day."

Nate chuckled. "You seeing this, Carter? This is the moment we all realize we peaked in high school."

"Not sure you ever peaked, Nate," I said, casually scanning the rest of the arrivals.

The super VIP crowd was trickling in. It wasn't just fans. This tour had attracted serious money.

I spotted a cluster of Korean businessmen stepping out of sleek black SUVs near the restricted entrance. Their movements were calculated, their suits crisp despite the heat.

These were the kind of men who didn't just attend concerts.

They funded them.

Security escorted them toward the private seating area, where top-tier corporate sponsors had the best seats in the house.

It wasn't just them, either.

There were younger guys in luxury streetwear—high-end sneakers, fitted jackets, sunglasses that probably cost more than my first car—who carried themselves with a blusterous exuberance that only a silver spoon could deliver.

I made a mental note to keep an eye on them.

"Chaebol kids," Jacob muttered with a groan. "Damn, I was hoping they wouldn't show."

I looked at Jacob. "Explain."

Jacob sighed, leaning in and lowering his voice. "Second- and third-generation heirs of Korea's biggest corporations—sons of CEOs, executives, politicians. Born into insane wealth. Never heard 'no' in their lives."

Jacob looked at me seriously. "They are pretty much either the love interest or the bad guys in most Korean dramas."

I raised an eyebrow. "You watching a lot of Korean dramas, Jacob?"

He shrugged. "Get with the times, Captain. Korean stuff is all the rage."

I glanced back at the group. They stood together, laughing easily, exuding effortless confidence, as if they knew the world belonged to them.

Jacob's voice carried irritation. "Some of them are decent,

but most are entitled as hell. They think everything's theirs for the taking—including people."

My eyebrow lifted. "You think they'll cause trouble?"

Jacob laughed bitterly. "Nova's here, aren't they? These guys lust after idols—especially ones at the top."

My jaw tightened slightly.

"Obsessed?" I asked.

"Worse than obsessed. It's a game. They date idols as trophies, flaunt them around, use their fame, then toss them aside when they're bored." He shook his head. "And if idols refuse them? Let's just say they don't handle rejection well. Money makes them think everything's for sale—or that they can pressure people until they fold."

I exhaled sharply, watching the group again. They looked like typical rich kids killing time before a show, but I knew better than to ignore warnings like this.

"Have they caused trouble before?" I asked.

Jacob shrugged. "Nothing officially proven. Money buries scandals. But enough rumors exist to know they're not harmless."

"Great," I muttered.

Jacob shot me a serious look. "Keep an eye on them, Carter. Especially with Ji-an around. She's hot shit right now."

I didn't visibly react, but something sharp and unwanted lodged itself in my chest.

Rich guys at events like this could go one of two ways— they could be respectful and low-key (I've met plenty of those; not all rich people are assholes) or they could be entitled pricks who believed that wealth made them immune to rules.

I'd seen both.

Then my attention shifted again, back to the group. They were starting to move, coming closer to our position. And that's when I saw her—I mean really saw her. She stood barely twenty yards away, suddenly in clear view as people parted.

Ji-an.

It shouldn't have surprised me.

I knew she was coming. Knew she was part of Nova.

But knowing didn't mean I was ready.

For a moment, I just stared.

How the hell was anyone supposed to get anything done around a woman like that?

Even in a casual outfit, she was eye-catching. Tall, long legs that went on forever. Dark, sleek hair shifting against her shoulders. Flawless skin, high cheekbones, full lips slightly parted as she took in her surroundings.

It wasn't just her beauty. I'd seen plenty of beautiful women.

It was the way she existed.

Like she had nothing to prove, yet could effortlessly take over the world.

I clenched my jaw, forcing myself back into work mode.

She wasn't the job.

She was just part of the job.

I had work to do.

But my initial assessment hadn't changed:

She was too pretty.

Even as I moved toward the next checkpoint, scanning for security gaps, I could still feel her presence behind me.

And when I glanced back—just once—I caught her staring.

Not at the view.

Not at the venue.

Not even at the pretty-boy VIPs already starting to swarm around her.

She wasn't looking at any of it.

She was looking… at me.

What the hell?

It was a long, steady look.

Her expression?

Annoyed.

Borderline angry.

Even from twenty yards away, I could feel it.

Wait—what?

Why was she glaring at me, of all people?

I shook my head and kept walking.

Just kept walking.

Maybe if I walked far enough, I could convince myself none of this mattered.

That she wasn't a big deal.

That she wasn't in my head.

Because she shouldn't be.

She was just another artist at another security gig.

Just another job.

Right?

The quiet didn't last.

I was still fuming quietly over Ji-an's irritated glare when Nate stiffened beside me, elbow nudging my ribs.

"Uh-oh," he muttered. "Trouble inbound."

I turned slowly. Heading toward us was a small group— three of those wealthy chaebol kids, swagger in full display.

I could already tell these fools were going to annoy me.

The last man, however, was different. Leading them was a tall, sharply dressed Korean guy in a tailored black suit and perfectly polished shoes. His dark hair was swept back, his face composed into careful neutrality. Unlike the others, he moved like someone who knew exactly what authority he wielded.

I recognized him instantly from the briefing files: Han Si-woo, head of Nova's personal security. A former Korean special forces officer. Reputation: ice-cold and utterly professional.

He stopped a few feet away, nodding curtly to me. "Mr. Carter."

I returned the nod calmly. "Mr. Si-woo."

His eyes flicked quickly to Nate and Jacob, clearly assessing my team before refocusing on me.

"These gentlemen," Han said smoothly, gesturing toward the wealthy young men, "are VIP guests. They've requested personal introductions with Nova."

Ahhh… now I get it.

I glanced at the trio, keeping my expression neutral. "No direct interactions before the show. That's the policy."

One of the young men laughed softly, stepping forward

with an easy, practiced smile. He was tall and lean, casually stylish in designer jeans and a dark silk shirt. Everything about him—from his carefully tousled hair to the confident tilt of his chin—spoke of privilege. He extended his hand.

"Lee Min-hyuk," he introduced himself casually. "I'm sure you understand—special circumstances. My family is one of Nova's largest investors. Just a quick hello, nothing intrusive."

His eyes shifted briefly toward Ji-an, lingering with open appreciation.

Something tightened in my chest, and I fought to keep my voice even. "Sorry, Mr. Lee. No exceptions."

Min-hyuk's smile sharpened, still polite but colder. "Maybe you don't fully understand who you're dealing with—"

I took a measured step closer. "I understand perfectly. Your investment grants you premium seating and VIP access after the show. Not private meetings. Not backstage passes. And certainly not direct access to the performers before their set. These are the rules that their agency set up for the tour. No exceptions. If you have a problem with it, take it up with the home office."

Han Si-woo's eyes narrowed slightly, but he didn't intervene immediately, silently weighing my response. Min-hyuk scoffed quietly, irritation cracking through his charming façade.

"You're overstepping, Mr. Carter," he said softly. "You're just venue security. Han-ssi here handles Nova. Maybe you should let him do his job."

I met Han's gaze steadily. "If you want to speak privately about protocol, we can. But these rules aren't negotiable, and you know it. Your CEO put them in place. Do you want to tell him we broke his rules for his son?"

Han held my stare a long moment. Finally, he exhaled slightly, turning to Min-hyuk with measured politeness.

"Mr. Lee, Mr. Carter's right. The rules are clear. I'm sure you understand."

Min-hyuk's jaw clenched. He clearly wasn't used to being denied. His two companions shifted uncomfortably, glancing toward me like they expected me to apologize, backtrack, or bow under the weight of his name.

Not happening.

Min-hyuk's expression cooled again, arrogance returning like armor. "Understood," he said quietly. His eyes slid back toward Ji-an, still standing in the distance, before returning pointedly to me. "We'll catch up after the show, then."

The words were calm, almost friendly. But the implied threat was obvious.

He turned, strolling off with casual ease. His friends followed, leaving a tense silence hanging behind them.

Han Si-woo exhaled slowly, turning fully to face me. "Thanks, Carter. You handled that firmly. Good."

I arched a brow. "You expected differently?"

Han's lips twitched faintly—an almost-smile. "No. But Min-hyuk isn't someone who takes rejection lightly. His family practically owns half of Seoul. He has influence but cannot go against his own father."

I held his gaze evenly. "He doesn't own The Gorge, and

we are only following the rules they established. Why set rules if you aren't going to follow them yourself?"

Han laughed. "And now you know the job of dealing with rich second generations!"

Han shook his head. "Thanks for handling it. Just be aware—he has his sights set specifically on Ji-an. I don't expect him to drop this quietly."

Something sharp twisted in my chest again, but I nodded once. "Noted. Thanks for the heads-up."

Han's expression shifted briefly, a fleeting look of understanding. Then it vanished, replaced by his usual, unreadable neutrality.

"Good luck tonight," he said coolly. "Let's keep things quiet."

I gave him a short, respectful nod as he moved off to rejoin Nova's entourage. Nate and Jacob both watched him leave, their expressions tense.

Jacob muttered quietly beside me. "This job just got a whole lot more interesting."

I sighed, already anticipating the headache ahead. "Understatement of the year."

But I couldn't deny it—I was bothered. Not by Min-hyuk's entitled attitude or his money. I'd dealt with worse.

No, it was the way he'd looked at Ji-an.

Like she was something he already owned. Something he could buy.

My jaw tightened again.

Not happening.

Not tonight. Not ever.

CHAPTER 11
JI-AN

THE MOMENT I STEPPED INTO THE DRESSING ROOM, THE controlled chaos began.

Stylists flitted around like precision-trained artists, unpacking their kits, laying out palettes, curling irons, and an endless assortment of accessories. Wardrobe assistants ran final checks on our outfits, fussing over every little detail.

This was routine.

This was normal.

I should have been relaxing into it, letting the transformation wash over me like usual.

But I wasn't.

I was fuming, still thinking about him.

I sat down in the makeup chair, letting my stylist start working through my hair, but my mind was locked on Logan Carter.

He saw me get off the bus. Knew I was looking at him. We even made freaking eye contact. And then?

He walked past me like I was nothing.

No reaction.

Barely an acknowledgment.

Barely a second look.

Just a polite nod, like I was any other celebrity. Like I was any other woman.

"You're almost too pretty," he had said once. *"How does anyone function around you?"*

Yet now he had the gall to walk past me like I was invisible.

It pissed me off more than it should have.

I wasn't arrogant enough to expect men to fall over themselves whenever they saw me. But I was used to attention. I'm embarrassed to admit it, but I expect men to pay attention to me, even when I don't want it.

Maybe this was karma?

Then I had a thought—he couldn't have forgotten me, right?

Sure, our conversation at the airport was almost a year ago, and it had only lasted a little while.

Okay, maybe conversation was a bit of a stretch. He had talked, I had listened, and I had pretended I didn't understand him.

Was he mad about that?

Still, I felt like we'd had a moment—enough that I was excited to see him again when I found out he'd be working this concert.

Enough that I had gone looking for him online.

Enough that I had spent the last ten months messaging

him under an anonymous account.

Enough that I had built him up in my head as something different.

But apparently, to him?

I was nothing special.

Me? Nothing special? The same girl he had once told was too pretty?

Did he actually mean that when he said it?

Or was I actually too pretty for him to even want to know me?

What's the American expression?

WTF??

I clenched my jaw, forcing my face to remain still as my stylist started pinning sections of my hair back.

Fine.

If Logan Carter was going to pretend I didn't exist—

Then I'd make damn sure he had no choice but to notice.

"Make my eyes pop," I told the makeup artist. "And my hair—sleek, but with a bit of volume. I want people to look."

The woman grinned. "Oh, I love your pure sex appeal look. You got it. We're definitely making people look."

From the other side of the room, Min-ji gave me a knowing glance. Jisoo just giggled.

"That 'people' wouldn't include Lee Min-hyuk, would it?" Min-ji said.

I almost gagged.

Lee Min-hyuk. A third-generation chaebol brat. His father was the CEO of our agency's parent company. His dad was the boss, basically. Lee Min-hyuk had been chasing me since my debut, and I had firmly rejected him.

He couldn't be here, could he?

"Lee Min-hyuk," I said flatly. "Why would I worry about him looking at me?"

Hye-won laughed from her chair. "He likes you, Ji-an. You're not going to be able to avoid him. You know that."

I refused to react.

"I just want to look my best," I said smoothly. "That's all. It has nothing to do with Lee Min-hyuk."

Min-ji smirked. "Sure. And I just think it's interesting that 'your best' suddenly requires extra glam."

Hye-won, always one to stir the pot, leaned in. "While we're on the topic, why were you staring at that security guard earlier?"

I froze. "I don't know what you're talking about."

She laughed. "Right."

I shot her a look. "I wasn't staring. I don't stare at boys. Especially ones that freaking ignore me."

Shit. Didn't mean to say that part.

"You definitely were," Min-ji confirmed. "You were staring so hard you almost tripped over your own feet."

"Don't be ridiculous," I muttered.

"I know what I saw," she countered.

Min-ji wiggled her eyebrows. "Not that I can blame you. I'm not into white boys, but that one was really cute. Very manly. Maybe we should ask around."

"Already did," Hye-won said with a smirk. "Believe it or not, he's the head of security for the event. Total badass. Military background. Apparently, he's kind of a big deal in this backwater town. Also, is it just me, or did he look familiar? Has he worked with our tour before?"

"I was just thinking that," Jisoo said. "I swear I've seen that guy before."

Min-ji contemplated.

"You three have weird taste," I said casually. "He's not even that good-looking."

"Oh, so you don't think he's cute?" Hye-won said. "Fine. Then I think I'll ask for his phone number. He looks aggressive—just my type."

"Oh! You're so bold," Min-ji said, giggling. "Perhaps I'll enter the mix too. He was really cute."

"I'm in," Jisoo added. "Same bet. First to get his phone number wins."

I ignored all of them and let the stylists work.

When I finally looked in the mirror, my reflection was lethal.

Dark, striking eyes, lined just right—the kind of look that could stop a man mid-sentence.

Lips full and softly painted, just enough to draw attention.

Hair sleek and controlled, framing my face with just the right amount of movement.

I looked dangerous.

I looked ready.

Let's see you ignore me now, Logan Carter.

CHAPTER 12
JI-AN

THE SECURITY OFFICE WAS TOO SMALL FOR THE NUMBER OF people crammed inside.

Nova's management team was there—handlers, publicists, and a few personal security staff seated around the long conference table. The members of Nova stood against the wall, waiting for the briefing to begin.

And standing at the front, beside the venue's manager, was Han Si-woo.

Shorter than Logan but broad-shouldered and sharp-eyed, Si-woo carried himself with the quiet confidence of a man who had been doing this for years. His suit was immaculate, his tie crisp, but there was nothing corporate about him. He had the air of a soldier—a bodyguard who had seen enough to know when things could turn south.

The room buzzed with chatter. The support crew talked animatedly while a few security guys leaned against the wall, watching a video on someone's phone. From the sound of it, they were playing a Nova performance clip.

I wasn't paying attention to any of it.

I was waiting.

Waiting for him to walk in.

Waiting to see if the extra time I'd spent making sure I looked like a goddamn goddess would get a reaction out of him.

The door swung open.

I didn't look up immediately.

But then—

The energy in the room shifted.

The quiet hum of conversation dipped.

And I felt it.

A presence.

Commanding. Confident.

I lifted my gaze—

And there he was.

Logan, not five feet from me.

Looking stupidly handsome.

Dressed in black tactical gear, radio clipped to his vest, sleeves rolled up just enough to show off his forearms. Sharp. Professional. Completely unfazed by the fact that he was in the same room as the woman he had once loudly declared was ridiculously attractive.

The one he was now ignoring.

The dick.

Si-woo was the first to speak.

"Carter." His voice was calm, measured, but there was an

unmistakable edge to it. His English was perfect, with zero accent. "Glad you could finally join us."

Logan didn't blink. "Some of the early arrivals are causing problems."

Si-woo's gaze flickered, a silent exchange passing between them. Then he nodded. "Urgent?"

"Not urgent. But disconcerting."

"I see." Si-woo scanned the room. "We'll discuss it later. Let's get started."

The venue director—John? Don? Bond? Something like that—cleared his throat. "Alright, for those of you who don't already know, this is Han Si-woo, head of Nova's private security team. He'll be working directly with Logan Carter, head of venue security, to ensure the group's safety throughout the event."

Logan gave a curt nod. "Nice to meet all of you."

Si-woo stepped forward. "I know what you're all thinking —Mr. Carter looks young to be leading an operation like this."

There was some murmuring among Nova's entourage. They were thinking it, even though Logan was in his thirties.

Si-woo's expression didn't waver. "I've read Mr. Carter's file. Former military. Private security consulting. Good credentials. He's also the CEO of Archangel Protective Services. This is his house."

The murmurs changed. I could tell from their faces— Nova's staff was impressed.

Si-woo turned to Logan. "You have their attention, Captain. It's your show."

Logan nodded, then addressed the room.

"Thank you, Mr. Han." His tone was even, professional. "I appreciate that Nova chose The Gorge as one of their venues. I understand this is your first time performing in central or eastern Washington, and I know your fans are excited. Thank you for being here—and for trusting Archangel Protective Services with your safety."

He gave a small, respectful bow. I liked that.

Logan continued. "Let's go over the security plan." He motioned toward the layout on the screen. "This is one of the largest outdoor venues on Nova's tour. We have multiple entry and exit points to monitor, along with VIP sections that require tighter control. Unlike an arena, there are no solid walls to keep threats at bay. The only structures providing real security are the administrative buildings. Vigilance is key. The summers here mean long daylight hours, but when it gets dark, it gets dark. Staying together—especially our stars —will be rule number one."

There were nods around the room.

Logan pointed to Si-woo. "Mr. Han's team will be covering the group directly, while my team will handle perimeter security, crowd control, and backstage access."

I barely heard any of it.

I was too focused on him.

The way he spoke. The way he commanded the room. The way he still hadn't looked at me.

Maybe I should throw something at him.

It was childish, but at least he'd have to acknowledge me.

I was standing right in front of him—the same girl he had

talked to for nearly an hour in an airport, the same one he had unknowingly been messaging for months—

And he was acting like I didn't exist.

This was worse than before.

He was ignoring me on purpose.

I folded my arms, barely hearing the rest of the briefing as Logan continued outlining safety measures, emergency protocols, and audience management.

All I could focus on was the fact that he still hadn't acknowledged me.

And the longer he kept that up?

The more I wanted to make him.

"Any questions?" Logan finally asked, glancing at Nova's team.

I saw my chance.

I let the silence stretch a second too long—then tilted my head and said, voice smooth as silk, "Hello, Mr. Carter. Thank you for keeping us safe."

Si-woo's gaze flicked to me immediately, picking up on something.

But Logan?

He barely reacted.

Just gave me a stiff, polite nod, his expression unreadable. "Ms. Ji-an. You're welcome."

That was it.

No second glance.

No flicker of recognition.

Nothing.

I clenched my teeth.

Fine. If he wanted to play it this way...

"I do have a question, Mr. Carter," I said, keeping my tone light. "Your team seems awfully standoffish. Will you be assigning personal security to each of the members in addition to our regular bodyguards? That's what most venues do. I assumed it was standard protocol."

Si-woo raised an eyebrow. He knew what I was doing.

Logan, on the other hand, didn't miss a beat. "No, we won't. We don't currently have any female security staff, and that was a requirement from your management."

Before I could stop myself, I said, "I don't think that's a good idea. I think you should assign individual guards for each of us. I'd feel much safer if you protected me personally."

The room went silent.

Si-woo's brows lifted slightly. My bandmates turned to look at me.

Logan's eyes finally met mine.

And for the first time since he walked in, I felt his attention.

There was a pause—a fraction of a second where something passed between us.

Logan's expression remained neutral, but I saw it. The flicker of something behind his eyes.

He recovered quickly. "I don't play favorites. I doubt you need my undivided attention," he said evenly. "Though I have to disagree with your basic premise, Ms. Ji-an."

He turned to the rest of Nova, then back to me. Then he smiled.

Its effect was devastating.

"If I'm being frank," he continued, "your staff is used to your presence. I'm not sure close proximity to you and my team is a good idea."

I narrowed my eyes. "Oh? And why is that, Mr. Carter?"

His smile didn't waver. "Because as professional as my staff is, I'd be surprised if anyone could fully focus in your presence."

A few chuckles rippled through the room.

Si-woo sighed.

Wait. WHAT?

Did he seriously just—

My face went red instantly.

I mumbled some half-response that didn't even make sense.

Logan raised an eyebrow, then turned back to the team. "Alright. If there's nothing else, let's get to work."

CHAPTER 13
LOGAN

THE SECOND THE MEETING ENDED, I STEPPED OUT OF THE cramped security office and into the hallway, inhaling deeply.

I needed a minute.

Just one damn minute.

Because whatever the hell just happened in there?

That wasn't normal.

I had worked security for celebrities before. I did security for several years before joining the Marines. Actors, musicians, VIPs, politicians—people who thought the world revolved around them. I had seen egos, seen the way people walked into a room expecting attention.

But Ji-an?

Ji-an didn't have to expect attention.

She commanded it.

Just by standing there.

And she knew it.

She'd taken her time getting ready for that briefing. I

wasn't blind. I noticed the way the other members of Nova had done their usual stage prep—getting their hair and makeup done, throwing on stylish but comfortable outfits.

And then there was Ji-an.

The woman was out of control.

She walked into that briefing like she owned the damn place—fitted black blazer over a cropped top that barely skimmed her ribs, long legs wrapped in sleek, high-waisted pants that made her look taller than she already was. Her hair was dark, glossy, perfectly styled—not effortless, but designed.

And her eyes?

Sharp. Lined just enough to be dangerous.

She was flawless in a way that shouldn't have been possible.

A woman like that shouldn't have existed in real life.

But she did.

And she was staring at me the entire damn time like I owed her money or murdered her puppy.

Not just looking. Watching.

Like she was waiting for me to react.

And I had.

Not outwardly. I am a professional, dammit. But inwardly? The second she started talking, my brain had short-circuited for half a second.

Because she hadn't just pushed me—she'd tested me.

And I had pushed back.

And then, for some stupid reason, I'd opened my damn mouth.

"Because I'd be surprised if anyone could fully focus in your presence."

That was what I had said.

Jesus and almighty Joseph, who talks like that? Why do I seem to stick my foot in my mouth every time I get around this woman?

I exhaled sharply, rubbing the back of my neck.

Ji-an was used to being admired, to being wanted. She had that lethal combination of power, beauty, and awareness of both. She was the kind of woman who could make a man lose his footing, his sense, and maybe even his damn dignity.

And I had given her exactly what she wanted.

Recognition.

Attention.

Hell, I had practically handed her a loaded weapon and dared her to use it on me.

But none of that mattered.

She wasn't my job.

Keeping her safe was.

I was about to push all of this out of my head and head toward the main staging area when a familiar voice broke through my thoughts.

"Logan. We got a problem."

I turned to see Mark, one of my senior security officers, jogging up the hallway, his expression tight.

Immediately, my brain shifted.

Business mode.

"Talk to me," I said.

"Things are getting weird. Obsessed fans." Mark exhaled.

"We caught two guys trying to sneak past the barricades into the VIP section. They had fake credentials, but that's not the part that worries me."

I frowned. "What does?"

Mark lowered his voice.

"We've been using that new AI program to monitor some of the online chatter in private fan groups. At first, it was the usual obsessive talk—stuff about getting close to the group, people bragging about sneaking into restricted areas. But there's one account that's been escalating."

My entire body tensed.

"Escalating how?"

Mark looked grim. "Threats. Weird ones."

That word hit like a rock in my gut.

"Not the usual 'I love you so much I want to breathe your air' kind of crazy," Mark continued. "This one's talking about making sure the purity of her sainthood remains undiminished."

Damn. A possessive. A weird one at that.

My stomach turned.

I'd seen this before.

There were different kinds of obsessed fans—the delusional ones who thought they were in a relationship with the celebrity, the ones who just wanted attention, the ones who crossed personal boundaries.

And then there were the possessives.

The ones who thought they owned the person.

The ones who got violent when reality didn't match the fantasy.

"How serious are we talking?" I asked, my voice tight.

Mark exhaled. "Could be nothing. Just another idiot talking big behind a screen. But the language is getting worse and freaking weird. And the two guys we caught outside? One of them follows that account."

My jaw clenched.

This wasn't just another concert.

This was a target.

I turned, my gaze sweeping toward the far end of the venue where the private dressing rooms were.

Where Ji-an was.

I was still frustrated with her, still irritated by whatever game she was playing, but none of that mattered.

Because none of it would mean a damn thing if I couldn't keep her safe.

"This guy have a name?" I asked.

"We're still digging," Mark said. "The account's been wiped clean a few times, but we're tracking the IP."

Before I could respond, another voice cut in.

"We are aware of the threat, and we already have a plan for that."

I turned to find Han Si-woo standing there, arms crossed, his expression unreadable.

Mark hesitated, then glanced at me before stepping back.

Si-woo exhaled. "You're worried. So am I."

I studied him. "How much do you know?"

"Enough," he said. "We've been tracking similar patterns across Korea, Japan, and Thailand. This isn't an isolated incident. Thus far, it's been all talk."

Of course they had.

I narrowed my eyes. "Then you already know what needs to happen."

Si-woo's jaw tightened. "Yes. Which is why I'm staying with the girls."

I frowned. "You personally?"

"They are my responsibility," Si-woo said simply. "I won't trust this to anyone else."

I studied him. "What aren't you telling me?"

He sighed. "You're way too young to be this sharp."

He looked at me cautiously. "We had an incident last year with one of our guards letting a VIP slip into a private space. They had some bad stuff planned for Ji-an and Jisoo. That's when we first found out about this group. They call themselves the Brotherhood. We were able to intercept, but it was close. The girls don't know anything about it."

"Ahh," I said. "Hence the rule for the female guard. You're trying to limit access to additional help."

He nodded. "Something like that. I know it's not a long-term solution, but the Nova hysteria is beyond even BTS and Blackpink. They're going into the record books. We have to keep them safe. Our national pride is on the line."

National pride. Okay, that seemed a bit over the top, but what do I know?

A flicker of something settled in my gut.

I nodded slowly. "Alright. But that means I run everything else. Perimeter, barricades, VIP crowd control, and your backups."

Si-woo held my gaze for a long moment. Then he nodded.

"Fine."

There was an understanding between us.

I wouldn't fight him on this.

But when shit went down?

It wasn't going to be up to him.

Because if anyone got close to Ji-an, Si-woo wasn't going to be enough.

And I had a bad feeling that moment was coming.

Soon.

CHAPTER 14
JI-AN

THE MOMENT WE STEPPED BACK INTO OUR DRESSING ROOM, THE energy shifted.

I barely had time to sit before Min-ji spun around, arms crossed, grinning like she had just uncovered the biggest scandal of the year.

"So," she drawled, "should we talk about the American?"

I sighed, dragging a hand through my hair. "I don't know what you're talking about."

"Don't lie," Hye-won said, flopping onto the couch like she was settling in for a drama. "You two were eye-sexing the entire meeting."

I nearly choked. "We were not."

"Oh, come on," Min-ji teased. "It was the most intense non-conversation I've ever seen. You two should get back to Seoul because you are both missing your true calling as K-drama actors."

She lifted her chin, doing a terrible impression of Logan's

serious, unimpressed expression. "'I don't play favorites, Ms. Ji-an.'"

Hye-won giggled. "And then you? 'Oh, but shouldn't you? Wouldn't it be safer if you were personally assigned to me?'"

I rolled my eyes. "I did not say that."

"You might as well have, right before you stripped naked and took him to bed."

"I was making a point."

"Oh, your point was very clear."

"You're impossible."

"You were flirting."

"That is ridiculous. I was testing him," I corrected, though the words felt weak even as I said them.

Because, okay—maybe I had been both.

Logan Carter had ignored me. Brushed me off like I was just another idol in a security briefing. He'd looked at me with that calm, unreadable expression, barely reacting, like I was just a job.

Like he hadn't spent an hour talking to me in an airport.

Like he hadn't spent the last ten months unknowingly messaging me online.

And I had wanted to shake him.

Make him crack.

Make him see me.

And for a second—just a second—I thought I had.

That moment when I pushed, and he finally looked at me. When I saw the flicker in his eyes, the hint of something buried under all that restraint.

But then?

He smiled.

And the bastard had said, "Because I'd be surprised if anyone could fully focus in your presence."

And I had felt that.

Like a direct hit to the stomach.

Like he was the one testing me.

I wasn't used to that.

I wasn't used to any of this.

And now I was dealing with Min-ji, Jisoo, and Hye-won smirking at me like I had just confessed to something scandalous.

"I don't care about Logan Carter," I said flatly.

Hye-won snorted. "Sure. That's why you spent the entire meeting glaring at him."

"I wasn't glaring."

"You were."

Min-ji grinned. "You looked like you wanted to either fight him or—"

"Finish that sentence, and I will kill you."

Hye-won laughed, but before she could say anything else, our manager, Seung-hwan, clapped his hands.

"Enough gossip," he said. "Let's focus."

He wasn't wrong—we had a concert to prepare for—but I could tell even he had noticed the shift in energy.

And then, right when I thought the conversation had died, Min-ji threw out one last parting shot.

"Well," she said, stretching dramatically, "if you don't care about Logan Carter, then I guess it won't bother you if I go find him after the show and ask for his number."

I did not throw a bottle at her.

I did not get irrationally irritated.

I did not care.

At all.

But when Min-ji laughed and ducked behind the couch, I might have started planning my revenge.

The concert had gone off without a hitch.

Well—mostly.

There had been a few overly excited fans near the barricades, but nothing out of the ordinary.

Except now, as I sat in front of the mirror, wiping away the last traces of stage makeup, I could hear Seung-hwan and some of the staff murmuring in the hallway.

Low voices. Serious tones.

I glanced at Min-ji, Jisoo, and Hye-won. They had heard it too.

The door opened. Seung-hwan stepped inside, his expression unreadable.

"What's going on?" I asked.

He hesitated.

Then, with a sigh, he said, "There was an incident tonight."

I put down my makeup wipe. "What kind of incident?"

He rubbed his temples. "Security caught two men trying to sneak in with fake credentials. It's not unusual—

plenty of fans try stupid things—but this time…" He hesitated.

Hye-won sat up straighter. "This time what?"

Seung-hwan exhaled. "One of them was linked to an account making threats against you, Ji-an."

A chill ran down my spine.

I swallowed. "Threats?"

Seung-hwan nodded grimly. "Yes, but nothing I believe to be serious."

The room went silent.

Min-ji's playful teasing from earlier was gone. Hye-won's smirk had disappeared. Jisoo looked contemplative.

For a long moment, none of us spoke.

Then, finally, I found my voice. "What did Logan say?"

Seung-hwan sighed. "This man takes his duty very seriously. He said this breach was unacceptable."

"So how is Logan handling it?" I asked.

Seung-hwan's eyes flickered with something unreadable.

"He's already increased security by calling in additional officers—off-duty cops," he said. "He didn't look happy when he found out. Like he took the breach personally."

I wasn't sure why, but something about that sent a shiver through me.

Not fear.

Something else.

Something I didn't want to think too hard about.

So instead, I nodded.

"Alright," I said. "Then let's focus on getting to the next city safely."

Seung-hwan looked relieved. "Good. Just—be careful, Ji-an."

And then he was gone, leaving the three of us in heavy silence.

I turned back to the mirror, staring at my reflection.

For all my earlier frustration, for all my irritation over Logan's cold professionalism, one thing was now crystal clear.

This wasn't a game.

This wasn't about whether Logan Carter noticed me or not.

This was real.

And not for the first time that night, I was glad he was here.

CHAPTER 15
LOGAN

THE INTERROGATION ROOM WAS DIM, STALE, AND HEAVY WITH the weight of bad decisions. Two men sat cuffed to bolted-down chairs—a wiry white American in his thirties, his lip split from where security had already handled him, and a younger Asian man, barely past twenty, his hands twitching against the cuffs.

They weren't scared.

Not the way they should've been.

They were excited.

Like they were part of something bigger. Something righteous.

I had seen that kind of fanaticism before. In different places. Under different names. And it never led anywhere good.

"You don't get it," the young one muttered, shaking his head like he pitied me. "You think you can just keep her from us?"

I stayed silent, arms crossed, watching.

They always talked.

They always needed to talk.

"She's sacred," the American said, eyes bright with something unhinged. "You can't taint her. You can't let the world taint her. That's not what She was meant for."

She.

Like she was some divine figure.

Some untouchable thing.

My stomach turned.

"Ji-an belongs to the Brotherhood," the younger one went on. "She is the Virgin Priestess."

What the hell are these fools talking about?

I didn't react. Didn't give them the satisfaction.

"She is life. She is love. She is purity. Purity is a gift," the American murmured, almost reverent. "A gift that you people don't respect. But we do. We know what must be done to protect her."

My fingers twitched.

I wanted to break this wackjob's jaw.

But I kept my stance relaxed, kept my expression impassive. Kept them talking.

Because fanatics didn't just act alone.

And then it happened.

The slip.

"You should take us to her. They said she'd be alone by now. All has already been set in motion. You're too late to stop them," the younger one scoffed, almost rolling his eyes.

The American snapped his head toward him.

"Shut up."

But it was already done.

The idiot had let it slip.

They.

Not we.

They.

My blood ran cold.

The younger one had just told me exactly what I needed to know.

They weren't working alone.

And someone else had already made it through.

The American must have realized it too because he leaned forward, smiling through his busted lip.

"You can't stop it," he said softly. "No matter how fast you run."

I moved before I thought.

My fist connected with his face so hard his chair skidded back against the floor.

He slumped forward, groaning, but I was already turning, already barking at Mark—

"Where is Ji-an?"

Mark straightened. "She and two others from Nova stepped out back, near the river overlook. Security's with them, but—"

I didn't hear the rest.

I was already moving.

Shoving open the door, flipping on my radio.

"Where is Ji-an?" My voice was sharp, cutting through the frequency.

The response was immediate, but not fast enough.

"Out back, near the river. No unusual activity."

Then the transmission cut off. In a very unnatural, very planned way.

Shit.

I was already sprinting.

Halls blurred past me.

My pulse a threat.

The words pounded in my skull.

You're too late.

Not if I had anything to say about it.

CHAPTER 16
JI-AN

THE AIR WAS COOL, THE NIGHT SETTLING OVER THE RIVER WITH A deceptive calm. I stretched my arms, breathing in deep, grateful for the fresh air after hours of rehearsals, press, and the show itself.

Min-ji and Hye-won stood beside me, chatting quietly. Jisoo had opted to stay inside, too tired to enjoy the break. A few meters away, Han Si-woo and two of his men kept a watchful distance. Their posture was relaxed, but I knew better—Si-woo was never off duty.

I didn't notice at first when the radio clipped to his vest crackled with Logan's voice—then cut to silence.

Si-woo did.

His head snapped toward the device, brow furrowing.

He tapped it once. Nothing.

Again.

Still nothing.

"Jin, Lee, check the frequency," he ordered, his voice calm but firm.

The two security officers immediately reached for their radios. One shook his head. "It's out. All of them."

That was when the unease set in.

Something was wrong.

I turned toward Si-woo. "What's—"

A noise.

A whisper of movement in the dark.

And then—

Shadows.

A group of figures emerged from the brush just beyond the river overlook.

Ten men.

No signs. No noise. Just movement.

Si-woo immediately stepped forward, placing himself between us and them. His men did the same.

One of the figures stepped into the moonlight.

He was tall, thin, his face pale and stretched tight over sharp cheekbones. His eyes gleamed with something that sent a chill up my spine.

Devotion.

"We've come to take her," he said, voice eerily calm. "She must be purified."

Si-woo's stance shifted. I had seen him fight before, seen the way he assessed threats. He was already calculating, already deciding how to break these men down.

"You picked the wrong night," he said. "Turn around. Walk away."

One of the fanatics—because that's what they were, I realized—laughed softly. "You don't understand," he murmured. "This isn't a fight. This is destiny."

Then he moved.

It happened fast.

Si-woo lunged first, striking before the man could fully advance. His fist cracked against the fanatic's jaw, sending him staggering. The man crumpled, but before his body even hit the ground, the others surged forward.

The fight erupted in an instant.

Si-woo's men engaged immediately. One lunged at an attacker, sending him and another man to the ground in a tangle of limbs. The other swung, landing a solid punch before a second fanatic grabbed him from behind, yanking him into a chokehold.

Si-woo was a force.

He moved fast, precise. A strike to the ribs. A knee to the chest. A vicious elbow to the temple that sent another attacker sprawling.

But there were too many.

One of them slipped past.

I felt hands grab my arm—cold, unshaking, reverent.

"Come with us," the man whispered, his grip tightening. "Let us save you."

I yanked back, heart slamming against my ribs, but before I could scream, Si-woo was there.

He caught the man by the wrist and twisted.

There was a sickening crack.

The fanatic screamed, dropping to his knees, clutching his

broken wrist.

Si-woo didn't hesitate. He turned, driving his foot into the man's chest, sending him sprawling.

I gasped, breath ragged.

Min-ji was clutching my hand, eyes wide. Hye-won was frozen in place.

But it wasn't over.

A blade flashed.

One of the fanatics rushed Si-woo from behind.

I shouted, but Si-woo spun just in time, catching the attacker's wrist mid-swing.

Then another came at him.

Si-woo let go of the first man, pivoting, landing a brutal punch across the second man's face.

But the first attacker recovered too fast.

The knife struck.

It sliced across Si-woo's side.

He barely reacted.

Didn't even flinch.

But I saw the way his muscles tensed.

The way his body slowed.

The fanatics knew it too.

They pressed in.

Si-woo fought harder. He landed another blow, then another, but his breathing had changed—just slightly.

One of the fanatics grinned. "Even you can't stop fate," he whispered.

Then three of them attacked him at once.

Si-woo staggered.

His knees buckled.

Another strike.

Then another.

A grunt of pain—low, sharp.

And then—

Si-woo went down hard.

He stumbled, his hand clamping against his side, fingers pressing against the growing stain of blood on his shirt. His two guards were already on the ground, unmoving.

And then it was just us.

Me. Min-ji. Hye-won.

Surrounded.

Five men still standing.

They closed in, slow, deliberate, like they had all the time in the world.

Min-ji grabbed my arm. Hye-won's breathing went shallow.

I held my ground, forcing my body to stay still. I wasn't going to give them the satisfaction of fear.

One of them—a gaunt, sharp-featured man—stepped forward. His eyes gleamed in the dim light, wide and feverish.

"You don't understand," he murmured, almost reverently. "We're not here to hurt you."

The knife in his hand told a different story.

"You're sacred," another one whispered, his voice hushed with awe. "You were meant for more than this."

"We've come to save you," the first one continued, taking

another step. "The world is corrupt, but you… You are still pure."

My stomach twisted.

I had dealt with obsessive fans before. People who cried, who begged, who thought they knew me.

This was different.

This wasn't admiration.

This was worship.

"You were never meant to be paraded around like this," another added. His eyes flickered to Min-ji and Hye-won. "They're distractions. The unworthy."

Min-ji inhaled sharply. I felt her fingers tighten on my wrist.

"You think you're safe," one of them murmured. "That these people can protect you."

His head tilted toward Si-woo, who was still struggling to breathe.

"But they don't understand. They don't know what you are."

I clenched my jaw. "And what exactly am I?"

They smiled.

All of them.

It sent a chill straight through me.

"The Virgin Priestess," the first man whispered. "Untouched. Pure. The world has tainted everything else. But you… You can still be saved."

I took a slow breath. "And how exactly do you plan to 'save' me?"

His grip tightened on the knife.

"By making sure no one else ever touches you."

A gunshot tore through the night.

The man closest to me jerked violently, his body snapping backward before he crumpled to the ground.

The others froze.

Then—

A figure crashed into them, a force of nature in black tactical gear.

A fist connected with a jaw. A body hit the pavement. Someone screamed.

And then—

Then I saw him.

Logan.

And he was hell itself.

CHAPTER 17
LOGAN

I DIDN'T THINK.

I just moved.

The first shot rang out, cutting through the night like a blade. The man closest to Ji-an jerked violently and crumpled, but I was already shifting, already calculating the angles. The rest were too close to my charges—too close for another shot.

I flipped on the safety, holstered the gun, and sprinted.

The second guy barely had time to register me before my fist met his jaw with enough force to shatter something. He hit the ground hard, unconscious before he even landed. I was already pivoting, stepping into the next strike.

The third man turned too late.

I caught him mid-motion, my elbow driving into his throat. His eyes bulged, and I wrenched his arm so hard something snapped. He screamed. I threw him to the pavement.

The fourth guy came at me with a knife.

I caught his wrist mid-swing, twisted—bone ground against bone—then drove my palm into his throat. He gasped, crumpling. I ripped the knife from his grip and slammed the handle against his temple.

Four down.

One left.

He hesitated.

I didn't.

I closed the distance before he could blink, launching a flying knee straight into his face. The impact sent him sprawling. I landed over him, my knee pressing into his throat.

His breath hitched. His hands clawed at my wrist.

"Did you think," I growled, voice low and lethal, "that I was going to let you touch them?"

He gagged, scrambling against my grip. His eyes burned with something fanatical, something completely untethered from reality.

"Blasphemy," he wheezed. "How dare you impede our holy cause? When the Virgin Priestess awakens her power, you will be punished."

I cut him off with a punch to the face.

He gasped, blood spurting from his nose.

"You think you're a savior?" I murmured. "You think you're righteous?"

His wild eyes darted to the others, sprawled and broken across the pavement. He tried to speak, but I squeezed just a little harder, just enough to make him panic.

"Listen to me very carefully," I said, my voice calm, quiet. "You make sure your whole group understands. If you or any of your Brotherhood comes near her again, I will find every last one of you and kill you."

His eyes bulged. He nodded frantically, choking.

I let go.

He slumped, gasping, but I was already standing, already scanning. My pulse was still a sharp, controlled rhythm—violence simmering just beneath the surface.

The girls were still there.

Still standing.

Ji-an was staring at me.

Wide-eyed.

Like she wasn't sure whether to be horrified or—

Or something else.

But before I could process that, I turned to Si-woo.

He was down.

His hand was pressed against his side, his fingers slick with blood. He was conscious and struggling to stay upright.

I crouched next to him.

"You're bleeding," I said flatly.

Si-woo exhaled sharply. "No shit."

I pulled a strip of cloth from my vest, pressing it against his wound. "How bad?"

He let out a slow, controlled breath. "Bad enough."

"You going to make it?"

Si-woo smirked, despite the pain. "Would hate to leave you alone with them." He nodded toward me, Min-ji, and Hye-won.

I snorted. "That'd be real tragic."

I tied off the bandage, studying him. He wasn't going to

die. Not tonight. But he wasn't walking out of here on his own.

I clicked on my radio.

"Carter, what the hell is happening out there?"

I pressed the button. "Situation's contained, we need to lock this shit down," I said evenly. "Get a team to the river overlook. Now. We have men down."

Static. Then, "Copy that."

I clipped the radio back onto my vest, then turned to the others, the bodyguards.

I checked them. Thank goodness, they weren't in immediate danger. Both were knocked out; they would need to be checked at the hospital.

I exhaled, finally turning to Ji-an.

She was still staring.

I stepped closer.

Her breath hitched.

"Ji-an," I said quietly.

She swallowed.

Then, finally, she whispered, "You came."

I didn't blink. Didn't hesitate.

"Always."

CHAPTER 18
JI-AN

THE MOMENT THE LAST MAN HIT THE GROUND, RELIEF WASHED over me like a crashing wave. But none of us moved.

We were too stunned.

Too rattled by the reality of what had just happened.

Logan stood in the aftermath, pulse steady, breath even, as if he hadn't just singlehandedly dismantled the men who had come for us.

But then—

Si-woo.

He was still down.

I turned just as Logan moved toward him, dropping to one knee beside him.

Si-woo's face was pale, his breathing slow but controlled. His hand pressed against his side, fingers slick with blood. His shirt was ruined, soaked in red.

Logan didn't hesitate. He yanked a strip of cloth from his vest and pressed it firmly against the wound.

Si-woo inhaled sharply, but his expression remained neutral, a thin sheen of sweat on his brow.

"You're bleeding," Logan said flatly.

Si-woo let out a slow, sharp breath. "No shit."

Logan exhaled through his nose, his movements quick but efficient as he tied off the makeshift bandage. His hands were steady, practiced.

"How bad?" Logan asked.

Si-woo clenched his jaw. "Bad enough."

"You going to make it?"

Si-woo smirked, despite the pain. "Would hate to leave you alone with them." He nodded toward me, Min-ji, and Hye-won.

Logan snorted. "That'd be real tragic."

Despite the tension, something about the way they spoke —so calm, so measured—kept me grounded. Logan talked into his radio, but I didn't hear him. He checked the other guards, but I couldn't move.

The situation wasn't over, but at least for now, we were alive.

For now, we were safe.

Then Logan was in front of us.

I barely had time to register it before Min-ji moved.

She launched herself at Logan first, arms wrapping around his waist, her whole body shaking as she sobbed into his chest.

Hye-won followed a second later, grabbing onto his arm, fingers clenching like she was afraid to let go.

I stood frozen, watching as my best friends—two of the

strongest women I knew—clung to Logan like he was the only solid thing in the world.

Honestly, for that moment, he was.

Because we had just been attacked.

We had been seconds away from something terrible.

And if Logan hadn't gotten there in time—

I swallowed hard.

He didn't move at first, his hands hovering awkwardly, as if he didn't know what to do. Then he sighed and wrapped his arms around them both, holding them steady.

His voice was low. Steady. Unshakable.

"You're okay," he murmured. "You're safe. I won't let anyone hurt you."

I should have said something.

Should have moved.

Instead, I just watched.

Watched as he protected us, even now.

Watched as he absorbed every ounce of fear, every tremble, without a single crack in his composure.

He wasn't panicked.

He wasn't shaken.

He had just destroyed five men, and now he was standing there, holding my best friends, making sure they felt safe.

Finally, his gaze flicked to me.

"Ji-an."

I exhaled.

"I'm fine," I said quickly, before he could ask.

His eyes lingered on me, sharp and assessing, as if he

didn't quite believe me. But before he could press, his radio crackled.

"Carter, the police are on their way. ETA five minutes."

Logan sighed, gently detangling himself from Min-ji and Hye-won, who refused to let go at first. He touched his radio.

"Good," he said. "We need to wrap this up before it turns into a shitstorm."

And that was exactly what it was about to become.

Because no matter what had just happened—no matter how real the danger had been—this was going to blow up.

There would be questions.

Headlines.

Speculation.

And the Brotherhood lunatics?

This wasn't the last we'd hear of them.

I knew it.

Logan knew it.

And judging by the way he clenched his jaw, he was already preparing for the worst.

By the time we got back to the dressing room, the atmosphere had shifted.

Logan guided Min-ji and Hye-won to the couch, where they nearly collapsed from exhaustion, their adrenaline crash hitting hard.

Jisoo fussed over them, a bottle of water in each hand.

Seung-hwan had arrived, pacing furiously as he took a call from Nova's legal team, his face dark with stress.

And Logan?

Logan was making tea.

I blinked, thrown by the contrast. A man who had just committed serious violence on five people was now standing at the minibar, casually steeping tea like we were about to have a nice, peaceful evening.

"You drink this?" he asked, glancing at me.

I frowned. "Yeah?"

"Good."

He set the steaming cups in front of us, then grabbed a chair and turned it around, straddling it as he faced us.

The room was silent except for the sound of soft, careful sips.

Then Logan spoke.

"Talk to me," he said. "Tell me everything you know."

I looked at him, confused. "About what?"

He tilted his head slightly, unimpressed. "Don't play dumb. About them. The Brotherhood."

I exhaled slowly.

"We've dealt with stalkers before," I admitted. "Crazed fans. But this?" I shook my head. "This is new."

Logan watched me carefully, waiting.

I hesitated, then admitted, "There have been messages. Strange websites with Kickstarters for seed money. They've been writing manifestos on blogs and fan accounts. Saying weird things, but we've always ignored them."

His jaw tightened. "Like what?"

I glanced at Min-ji and Hye-won. They were quiet, letting me speak.

"Mostly about purity," I said finally. "Like…how I'm

supposed to be some 'symbol' or some shit. How I belong to them."

Logan exhaled, slow and sharp.

"That's why they were saying that outside," I realized. "The whole 'Virgin Priestess' thing."

Min-ji shuddered. "That's so messed up."

"Yeah," Logan muttered. "It is."

For a second, the room fell silent again.

Then he stood.

"We need to get you out of here," he said.

I blinked. "What?"

He grabbed his radio. "Mark, I want the cars pulled around back. Now."

"What about the police? They need your statement."

"Tell Sheriff Tate that he can call my cell. The girls need to get out of here. There might be more of these asshats around."

"Copy, Captain."

I frowned. "Logan—"

"This venue isn't safe anymore," he interrupted. "I don't care what the police say. You're leaving. Now."

His voice left no room for argument.

And for the first time in my life?

I didn't want to argue.

CHAPTER 19
LOGAN

I had one job.

Get them out.

No press. No attention. No more opportunities for psychos with knives.

The rest of my team stayed behind to handle the police, the venue, and the inevitable fallout. I took them—the ones that mattered—put them in unmarked cars, and got them the hell out of there.

No flashy black SUVs with presidential-level security that would tip off every stalker and tabloid in the city. Just normal cars, part of a normal convoy, heading back to Moses Lake like nothing had happened.

Because as far as I was concerned?

Tonight was over.

The only thing that mattered now was getting them back to the hotel, locking it down, and making sure nothing else touched them.

Ji-an hadn't fallen asleep.

She sat quietly beside me, arms wrapped around her knees, staring out the window.

Then, softly—so softly I almost missed it—

"Thank you."

I didn't answer right away.

Didn't trust myself to.

So I did what I always did.

I kept driving.

Kept my eyes on the road.

Kept moving forward.

Because if I let myself think about what had just happened?

I wasn't sure I'd be able to stop.

CHAPTER 20
JI-AN

By the time we pulled up to the hotel, exhaustion had settled deep in my bones. I wasn't alone—Min-ji and Hye-won were so out of it they were snoring, and despite myself, I laughed. It was so un-idol-like. Not that I could blame them. Even Jisoo, who hadn't been attacked, was fast asleep.

Logan parked the car smoothly, but when he cut the engine, no one moved.

I sighed, rubbing my eyes, turning in my seat and nudging Hye-won. "We're here."

She groaned in response.

Min-ji buried her face deeper into the car seat, mumbling something incoherent.

Only Jisoo stirred, immediately getting out of the car.

I glanced at Logan, expecting him to say something sharp and commanding, but he just stared ahead, jaw tight, fingers still gripping the steering wheel.

He was still in work mode.

Still scanning.

Still thinking like the soldier he was.

"Logan," I said, my voice softer than I expected.

His head turned slightly. "Yeah?"

"We should go inside."

For a second, he didn't move. Then he exhaled, unclipped his seatbelt, and stepped out of the car.

I pushed open my own door, stretching stiff muscles as I stood.

Then I heard a low, irritated grunt. I turned just in time to see Logan pulling open the back door, taking in the scene inside.

Min-ji hadn't moved.

Hye-won had—barely. She sat up a little, blinking blearily at Logan. "Five more minutes," she murmured before flopping back down.

Logan sighed through his nose. "That's not happening."

Min-ji let out a soft, dramatic snore.

He pinched the bridge of his nose and tried to give a little nudge.

I crossed my arms. "You can just shake them awake."

"Tried that," he said flatly.

I frowned. "You barely touched her."

Logan wasn't a man who tried. He *did*.

And apparently, in this moment, what he *did* was scoop Min-ji up into his arms, cradling her close to his chest. She snuggled in instinctively.

My eyebrows shot up.

So did my irritation.

"Seriously?" I muttered.

"What?"

"You're carrying her?"

"We can't leave her in the car now, can we?" He shifted her in his arms, completely unbothered. "You want to carry her instead?"

I gritted my teeth.

It wasn't that I wanted to carry Min-ji, and of course, we needed to hurry. And I knew I shouldn't be irritated. But Logan was handling her like she was some delicate, breakable thing, and it bothered me.

Logan gave me an amused smile and Min-ji an affectionate glance.

I glared. He hadn't looked at me like that. He was treating her like a freaking princess. He hadn't treated me like a princess.

What's up with that?

I exhaled sharply. "Fine. But you're not carrying Hye-won too."

"Why would I carry Hye-won?" he said dryly.

Jisoo didn't say anything—just laughed.

Hye-won was already dragging herself out of the car, rubbing her eyes. "No fair! Why does only Min-ji get princess carried?"

Min-ji, meanwhile, had fully relaxed against Logan's chest, breathing evenly.

I rolled my eyes. "She's going to be so embarrassed when she wakes up."

Logan smirked slightly. "What a silly thing to be embarrassed about. You can tell her I thought she was adorable."

I could feel the steam coming out of my ears. It took all my willpower not to throw my phone at him.

We headed inside, avoiding the main entrance, taking the service elevator straight up to our floor.

The moment the doors closed, I finally let myself breathe.

It was over.

We were safe.

For now.

Hye-won collapsed onto an oversized recliner. Logan set Min-ji down carefully on the couch, pulling one of the hotel blankets over her. She didn't even stir. He found her a pillow and made sure she was comfortable. He also checked her forearm like he was checking her temperature.

"She probably has a mild case of shock," he said more to himself.

Logan stepped away from Min-ji and leaned against the wall.

Jisoo and I both sat in chairs next to the couch.

For a second, none of us moved.

Then Hye-won sat up suddenly. "Unnie, can I stay here? I don't want to sleep alone."

I frowned. "What?"

"I don't want to be by myself." She looked at me, then at Jisoo, then Min-ji. "What if they're not done? What if someone else tries something?"

I hesitated.

Because she had a point.

Min-ji shifted slightly in her sleep, murmuring something under her breath.

Then, without even opening her eyes, she mumbled, "We should all stay together."

Hye-won nodded immediately. "Agreed."

Jisoo didn't say anything and simply nodded.

I sighed, running a hand through my hair. "Fine. You both can stay here."

Hye-won smiled in relief, already kicking off her shoes.

Then I turned to Logan.

"You should go," I said.

He didn't move.

Didn't blink.

Just stood there, arms crossed, watching me.

"Not happening," he said.

I narrowed my eyes. "You don't have to babysit us."

"No," he agreed. "But I do have to make sure you're safe. Until you leave this hotel, you're my responsibility."

I exhaled, frustration curling in my chest. "Logan—"

"Just let him stay," Hye-won muttered, already half-asleep. "I feel safer with him here."

I turned back to her. "You would?"

But she wasn't listening anymore.

Min-ji made a sleepy noise of agreement.

I sighed.

Logan just raised an eyebrow, like he knew he had won.

I scowled.

"Fine," I muttered, flopping onto the bed. "But you better not hover."

His lips twitched, like he was holding back a smirk.

"I'll try my best."

Somehow, I didn't believe him.

The hotel suite had finally gone quiet.

Min-ji was curled up on the couch, completely passed out under a thick blanket. Hye-won and Jisoo had claimed the bed in the second room, their whispered conversations fading into soft, even breaths as exhaustion overtook them.

That just left me and Logan.

I sat at the edge of the couch, legs tucked under me, my fingers absently running over the fabric of my sleeve. Across the room, Logan was leaning back in one of the dining chairs near the window, arms crossed, posture deceptively relaxed. He had dressed down some. Taken off his tactical vest, his shirt was pretty torn up; there were knife marks and rips in the fabric from the fight.

Seeing it made me realize how dangerous the situation had been.

Logan was breathing deeply, steady and alert. His eyes were still scanning the room, flickering to the doors, the windows, the shadows in the corners. Like he was still waiting. Still expecting something to go wrong.

I turned my head toward him. "Why did you pretend you didn't know me?"

Logan didn't react right away. Just let out a slow breath, like he'd been expecting the question.

"You should sleep."

I ignored that.

"Logan."

He exhaled, dragging a hand down his jaw. "Seriously? That's what you want to talk about?"

"Yes."

His mouth twitched slightly.

Then he met my eyes. "I wasn't pretending."

I scowled. "That's bullshit."

He let out a short laugh. "You are freaking adorable."

I glared. "You knew damn well who I was—am. Why did you pretend you didn't? We met at the airport in Hong Kong. We talked for almost an hour."

Logan tilted his head slightly. "Did we?"

I opened my mouth.

Then hesitated.

Because… technically, no.

At the airport, he had done all the talking. I had listened. I had wanted to see his gun magazine because I was too much of a coward to buy it myself and instead asked him to see his copy. But I did it in Korean. Before I corrected my mistake and spoke to him in English, he had started talking. I had let him ramble about whatever thoughts came into his head. I had played the amused, quiet stranger, laughing at his musings, nodding along, never offering anything in return.

And then I left.

He hadn't seen me since.

For almost a year, we had not met. We hadn't talked. At least as Logan and Ji-an. But I couldn't exactly say that now, could I?

I clenched my jaw stubbornly. I knew it was ridiculous. He didn't have any reason to "know" me. It still pissed me off. He should know it's me. Should know that I am Jess and that we are friends. Idiot.

"You still remembered me."

Logan exhaled through his nose. "I remember meeting a pretty girl at an airport. I remember talking to someone who I thought couldn't talk back. I remember saying a bunch of things that many might find embarrassing. I later found out she was famous just before she walked off, never to be seen again. Okay, that is a bit of a stretch, because I see you everywhere, all the time, but you get my point."

His eyes flickered, searching mine.

"You," he said, voice quieter now, "are Ji-an of Nova—a global superstar. A woman with millions of fans. A face on billboards, in magazines, on flashing screens. We spoke briefly on a random day, in a random city on a random trip. So why, exactly, would I assume you'd remember me?"

I opened my mouth.

Then I closed it.

Because I didn't have an answer.

Not one I could say.

Not the truth.

I couldn't tell him that I had never forgotten him.

That I had searched for him online.

That I had spent the last ten months talking to him as someone else.

That I had befriended his sister and joined the groups he liked.

That I had built him up in my head as something different.

Something more.

My stomach twisted.

I hated that he was making sense.

I hated that I suddenly felt stupid for expecting anything else.

Logan watched me carefully.

He was waiting.

I knew I should say something.

But I couldn't.

Logan smiled a very smirky smile. "The truth is I know *of* you. The whole bloody *world* knows of you. But I am a normal guy, an American, not into your brand of music, and I made an ass out of myself during the one interaction we had. Your exit wasn't exactly forgettable. Of course I knew— know who you are *now*. But that doesn't mean that I *know* you. And I certainly don't think it was appropriate to act familiar."

I looked away, exhaling sharply. "You're annoying."

Logan smirked. "And you're blushing."

I shot him a glare. "You think you're so clever."

"Pretty much."

"It's annoying."

"You said that. I wonder why you constantly seem upset with me."

I tried not to meet his eye.

He just sat there, watching me with that unreadable expression, like he was still trying to figure me out.

Ugh. He was so freaking smug; it almost made me mad that he was trying to figure me out.

Almost.

CHAPTER 21
JI-AN

LOGAN DIDN'T LET THE CONVERSATION DROP.

Of course, he didn't.

The man had the persistence of a soldier on a mission—because, in his mind, everything *was* a mission. That much I had gleaned from our conversations. And apparently, figuring out why I was mad at him all the time had just become his newest objective. I should have known he wouldn't let it go.

He leaned forward slightly, resting his elbows on his knees, gaze locked onto me. "So tell me something."

I sighed. "What now?"

"If we only met briefly almost a year ago, and considering I'm not exactly memorable," he said, voice even, measured, "why do *you* remember *me*? And better yet, why do you care so much that I remember you?"

My breath caught. He wasn't being cocky. He wasn't fishing for compliments or trying to trap me.

He was genuinely asking.

Because in his mind, he wasn't memorable. He shouldn't be on my radar.

Logan Carter. The man who had just single-handedly taken down five attackers like they were nothing, who commanded every room he walked into, who had unknowingly been living in my head for ten months... didn't think he was worth remembering.

I swallowed, looking away. "I don't know."

His eyes stayed on me. "Yeah, you do."

I clenched my jaw. "I don't."

"You're lying. And you're terrible at it."

I exhaled sharply, scowling. "You're so annoying."

That damn smirk, just barely there. "You've mentioned that."

I groaned, pressing my fingers to my temples. "You are such—"

I stopped.

Stopped, because I had almost said it. Almost blurted out, *You are such a know-it-all; no wonder Emily gets mad at you all the time.*

But I caught myself just in time.

My heart pounded. I had never slipped before. Never even come close. No one knew about me and Logan and how I basically stalked him.

But right now, sitting across from him, exhausted, irritated, and too caught up in the moment, I almost gave myself away.

Logan noticed the pause. His brows pulled together slightly, like he knew I had almost said something else.

So I did what I always did.

I covered it.

"You're the most obnoxiously persistent man I've ever met," I finished smoothly. "That's why I remember you. You don't shut up."

Logan exhaled a short laugh, shaking his head. "You're so full of shit."

My stomach twisted.

I hated how easily he could see through me.

Hated how much I wanted to prove something to him.

Hated that he was making me feel things I didn't want to feel.

So I did something reckless. Bold.

I pushed off the couch, walking over to where he sat.

His brows lifted slightly, but he didn't move as I crossed the room. He didn't move as I sat down—on his lap. He didn't move as I wrapped my arms around his neck, as I leaned in close, as I blew against his ear.

I tilted my head, watching him.

He was so *still*, so *controlled*. It irritated me. I wanted to see that control snap, to watch his composure crack, just a little. Just enough.

Slowly, deliberately, I let my fingers trail along the back of his neck, nails barely grazing his skin. He was warm beneath my touch, the heat of him seeping into my fingertips. His pulse was steady, maddeningly even.

I leaned in, my lips hovering just over his ear, close enough that I knew he could feel my breath against his skin. "You know," I murmured, my voice low, teasing, "I've been thinking..."

No real reaction. Zero change to his face. Only a barely-there shift, the tension in his shoulders tightening ever so slightly.

Encouraged, I pressed in closer, my chest just barely brushing against his. "You act so unbothered," I continued, my tone laced with amusement, "as if nothing gets to you. Like you don't even notice who or what I am."

I traced slow circles against the back of his neck, letting the silence stretch between us, thick with unspoken things.

I looked him right in the eyes; I held it there for a long moment. Then, softer, more dangerous:

"Tell me, Logan." My lips almost touched his ear now, a whisper away. "If I asked you to take me now, would you?"

A beat.

Then—

Logan hummed, tilting his head slightly like he was actually considering it. "Take you where?" His voice was maddeningly casual. "Depends. It's kinda late and I'm tired?"

I narrowed my eyes. "You know what I mean."

His lips quirked. "Do I?"

I exhaled sharply, dragging my nails a little harder against his skin, just to see if I could make him crack. "You are so—"

"Annoying?" His tone was so smooth, so effortlessly teasing, it made me want to strangle him.

I leaned in again, my lips barely brushing the shell of his

ear this time. "I'm asking if you want to have sex with me, Logan."

Logan didn't react right away.

Didn't shift. Didn't lean in.

Just watched me.

His gaze flickered, slow, controlled. From my eyes to my lips, then back again.

His jaw clenched.

The air between us tightened.

My palms were sweaty.

What did I just do? Did I seriously just invite Logan Carter to my bed?

Would he take me up on the offer? Take me to the bedroom and have his way with me?

I wasn't sure what I expected, but I wasn't ready for the way he inhaled. I wasn't ready for the heat in his eyes or the way his fingers twitched, like he was physically stopping himself from reaching for me.

I swallowed. For a moment—just a moment—Logan Carter didn't look like a man. He looked like a beast. A wolf staring down his prey.

And from that look, I expected our clothes to come flying off. I expected to be in his arms, calling his name, his hands on me, his mouth claiming mine.

I was ready.

But it didn't happen.

I watched as Logan felt his emotions. I saw them flicker across his face, raw and unguarded.

I watched as the beast slipped away.

As he controlled himself.

He didn't blink. Didn't move. Didn't lean in.

He was a statue—until he wasn't.

His hands came to rest on my thighs, light but firm. The touch was electrifying.

I nearly moaned.

His fingers shifted, tracing upward, higher and higher. My breath hitched. My throat went dry. I was half a second away from throwing caution to the wind and taking what I wanted.

And then he stopped.

Slowly, deliberately, he pulled his hands back, sat up a little straighter, and met my gaze.

For what felt like forever, he just looked at me.

Then, with the same steady, *infuriating* calm, he asked, "Why?"

I frowned. "What?"

"You just asked if I wanted to have sex with you."

"Yes."

"Why?" he repeated.

I hesitated.

Logan tilted his head. "Is this because I saved you?"

I scoffed. "Oh, come on."

"I mean, it's an easy conclusion." He shrugged, voice even. "I swoop in, take out the bad guys, you get a rush of adrenaline, and suddenly you think you want me. Classic."

I scowled. "That's not—"

I stopped.

Because, honestly? That wasn't entirely wrong.

Was it part of it? Maybe.

But it wasn't all of it.

Logan leaned back, stretching his legs slightly. I looked at his face; his expression was maddeningly unreadable. I adjusted myself on his lap. He didn't react.

"What if I said that it was?" I said. "What if I said that I find you attractive and that I am thankful and I want to use your body to comfort me?"

"I am not exactly soft. I should get you a cinnamon roll. Now that is comfort."

"Logan. I'm pretty sure I just asked you to take me to bed."

"Oh trust me. I caught that," he mused, that cocky smirk back in place, "and I must say, isn't this really bold for a K-pop idol? Trying to sleep with a man she doesn't even like?"

My scowl deepened. "I didn't ask you to marry me; I just asked if you wanted to join me in my bed. Apparently, you think I cannot be casual. And who says I don't like you?"

He smirked. "You've called me annoying like fifty times."

I rolled my eyes. "What are you, twelve?"

"I do love chocolate milk."

"Seriously, you're acting ridiculous."

"Am I?"

"Yes."

"You sure you're not just testing me? Trying to exercise control over the situation?"

"Why are you taking this so seriously?"

He just grinned. It made him look younger. Handsome. Freaking bastard.

Fine.

You want to play games.

You want to act like you're in control and don't care that I'm sitting on your lap practically throwing myself at you? I am going to prove it. I will get you to unleash the beast.

I took Logan's face in my hands, caressing his cheeks, feeling the stubble on his face. I ran my thumb across his lips.

"Take what you want, Logan," I whispered.

I leaned in to kiss him, but right before our lips met—

He shifted and then *flicked* my forehead!

It actually hurt.

I jerked back and gawked at him, stunned.

Did that just happen?!

This man rejected a bed invitation, my kiss attempt—and then flicked me in the forehead?!

I felt embarrassed. Then rage. Pure, unfiltered rage.

I shot up from his lap, glaring at him. He sat there, completely unaffected, like he hadn't just committed an unforgivable crime.

"What the hell was that?!"

He smirked. "Just checking to see if you were still awake."

I gasped. "You flicked me!"

"Yes."

"Ji-an. Leader of Nova."

"I'm well aware of who you are."

"I am one of the most famous women in the world."

"That is probably true."

"Are you out of your mind??"

"No, I am completely in control of my faculties."

I gave him an incredulous look. "So Ji-an from Nova *invites* you to her bed and then goes to kiss you, and *your* reaction is to flick her forehead? You *must* be insane."

Logan narrowed his eyes. Stood. He walked toward me aggressively. I panicked. I don't know why, but I found myself backing up. Suddenly, I was against the wall. Right before I touched the wall, I put my hands out like I was going to push him away. Somehow, and I don't know how, in one smooth motion, Logan grabbed both my hands in one of his, and suddenly my arms were above my head and my back was against the wall with Logan's body *almost* against mine.

We stood and stared at each other. Logan's other hand was on my hip, rubbing it. I could feel the heat of it. It made me shiver.

My breathing grew heavy as we locked eyes.

It was one of the sexiest things I have ever experienced.

I went weak in the knees. I had no idea how I was still on my feet. I continued to stare at Logan. And lord help me, I didn't know if I was scared or horny. Logan's eyes pierced me.

"Ji-an."

"Yes?"

"I flicked you because I needed to remind you that actions have consequences and you weren't thinking about yours."

Wait? What? What the hell did that mean?

Logan took his hand from my hip and touched my cheek. Then ran his fingertips across my lips and down my neck, slowly touching me just above my chest. He leaned in, and I thought he was going to kiss me, but then—

"Don't play these games; not everyone is as nice as I am."

Logan released me and took a step back, and I was left with my eyes closed for half a second. I didn't even realize that I had closed them.

Then I got pissed.

"You freaking bastard," I said, trying to keep my voice low so I didn't wake up the others. "You are the most arrogant, condescending, annoying man—"

"Careful," he murmured, eyes glinting. "You wouldn't want to hurt my feelings..."

"You just threw away a once-in-a-lifetime opportunity." I seethed. I needed to leave before I threw something at his stupid, smug face. I turned sharply on my heel, stomping toward the master bedroom. "I hate you,"

I muttered under my breath, slamming the door shut behind me. I collapsed onto the bed, furious, flustered, and incredibly turned on. The asshole actually rejected me and flicked me in the forehead.

ME???

I swore I heard him chuckle from the other room.

CHAPTER 22
JI-AN

I woke up way too early the next morning. My thoughts went instantly to the asshole out on my couch.

Logan. I should go out there and kick him. Or kiss him. Maybe both.

I wasn't sure what horrified me more: the fact that I had invited Logan Carter to bed last night or that he had actually rejected my advance.

I gritted my teeth, staring at my reflection in the mirror.

The bathroom was quiet, the dim morning light filtering through the frosted glass. I pressed my fingers to my temples, trying to process how the hell I got here.

I had never—*never*—thrown myself at a man like that before.

Sure, I'd flirted, teased, played with attraction when it suited me. I knew how to work a room, how to command attention, how to make men weak with a look.

But last night?

That had been different.

I sat on his lap. I had leaned into him, whispered in his ear, given him every possible invitation to take what I was offering.

And Logan Carter had rejected me.

Not just rejected me.

He had flicked me in the forehead.

I groaned, burying my face in my hands.

What was wrong with me?

I should be furious. I should be humiliated. And I was. But the worst part? The part I refused to admit even to myself?

I was also relieved.

For two reasons. One, I am not actually that experienced when it comes to intimacy. I am by no means a maiden, but I am not a very casual person. Acts of intimacy should be within the bounds of something—love? Marriage? A committed relationship. Something.

I am not sure what had come over me to be so bold and direct.

The second, and more importantly, Logan had done the thing no other man had ever done.

He had called me out.

He hadn't let me play games. Hadn't let me use attraction as a distraction or a means of control. Hadn't fallen over himself to impress me. Hadn't let lust take over and have his way with me.

He had looked at me. *Really* looked at me and understood my intentions, or lack thereof, better than I did.

And when I hadn't been able to answer him why…

He had seen through me.

I exhaled sharply, staring at my reflection like it might give me an answer I didn't have to a question I wasn't sure I wanted to ask.

So… what the hell am I supposed to do now?

The most F-ed up thing about this? If Logan had *wanted* me, if he had reacted, even a bit? Would I have denied him? I pictured his hands on my hips, his fingers caressing my cheek, my throat, my chest. I felt my face flush.

Would I have stopped Logan if he made a move? If he had taken what he wanted?

I am scared of the answer.

Still reeling, I stepped out of the bathroom, trying to shake off the memory.

Trying to forget the way Logan's hands had felt on my thighs. Trying to forget that, even when he rejected me, it had still made my skin burn.

And then I heard it.

"Oh my—"

Jisoo's voice.

Sharp. Alarmed. Then, chaos.

I stepped into the living room and stopped dead in my tracks.

Min-ji.

Snuggled against Logan.

No. Not just snuggled. Practically wrapped around him. Like a lover.

And Logan?

His shirt was open.

At some point in the night, Min-ji had gripped his already ruined shirt and opened it even more. The fabric was hanging loose, exposing a ridiculous amount of skin.

And Logan, of course, was still asleep.

Like the whole world wasn't falling apart around him.

Jisoo gasped dramatically. "Oh. My. Giddy Aunt."

Hye-won giggled. "That's insane."

I stared.

I had seen Logan fight. I had felt his strength before.

But this? This was outrageous.

Logan's body was magnificent. His entire torso was a map of carved muscle—defined abs, broad shoulders, deep scars scattered across parts of his skin. Not messy, not excessive—just powerful.

Sexy as hell.

This was the kind of body that didn't come from vanity.

This was the kind of body that came from experience.

Min-ji, still asleep, let out a soft sigh and nuzzled closer.

Her hands wandered over his chest and stomach, tracing abs like she was dreaming about it.

There was no way she was still asleep!!

Jisoo choked.

Hye-won slapped my arm. "Are you seeing this?"

Unfortunately, I was. And I hated it.

I forced my voice to stay even. "It's not a big deal; it's just a chest and, uh, abs."

Hye-won scoffed. "Not a big—are you blind? Look at his body! This is totally unfair. First, she gets a Princess Carry and—why does Min-ji get to sleep with Logan? I want to touch his abs!"

Jisoo nodded furiously. "Yeah, Ji-an, I get that you're jaded or whatever, but even you have to admit how crazy hot that is."

I did admit it.

Silently.

To myself.

Because it *was* crazy.

Because it *was* unfair.

Because it *was* infuriating.

Min-ji shifted again, her fingers *twitching* against Logan's stomach. Then—

Her eyes snapped open.

She blinked once.

Then twice.

And then, when realization hit—

She launched herself off him so fast she nearly fell off the couch. She wrapped her arms around her chest like she was trying to hug herself.

"Oh my—" She stumbled, tripping over the blanket. "I— what—how did—"

Logan finally stirred, frowning as he blinked up at the commotion.

He yawned and stretched. His torso flexed. "Good morning, why do you all look like someone murdered your cats?"

Min-ji clutched the blanket to her chest, eyes wide, face burning red.

Jisoo and Hye-won were dying, cackling behind their hands, trying to stifle their laughter.

I just crossed my arms, seething.

Logan, still groggy, exhaled slowly. "What's going on?"

Jisoo gawked. "Nothing, we were just realizing how much farther Min-ji is. I am super impressed."

Hye-won giggled. "I will not fall behind again."

Min-ji squeaked and turned her back to him like she couldn't bear to look. "I—I don't know how that happened!"

I wanted to yell at my bandmates for all of them to suffer for having thoughts about Logan. But I was too busy trying to ignore how *annoying* Logan was.

The way he was still half-sprawled on the couch, completely unbothered, his abs and chest right there, like he didn't even care that he had practically been molested in his sleep.

I turned away before my irritation showed on my face.

"You," I said tightly, "need to get dressed."

Logan blinked at me.

Then, as if finally processing that he was practically bare-chested, he grinned.

"You're so bold, Min-ji," he said lazily. "I find that immensely attractive."

Min-ji died on the spot.

She let out a strangled squeak before burying her face in the couch pillow.

Jisoo gasped dramatically, smacking my arm. "Shameless! Logan. You are so shameless!"

Hye-won grinned. "You are the worst."

And Logan?

He just stretched again, rolling his shoulders, looking completely unconcerned. He flexed his abs and chest muscles.

Hot damn, was it sexy.

I narrowed my eyes. I wanted to kill him.

Instead, I clenched my jaw, watching as he casually got up, rolled his shoulders again, and walked nonchalantly toward the bathroom.

Like he hadn't just caused a full meltdown in the room.

Like he hadn't just rejected me last night, but somehow ended up with Min-ji in his arms instead.

Yep. I was going to kill him.

As soon as he was gone, Jisoo shook her head. "Unreal."

Hye-won sighed dreamily. "I vote to adopt Logan as a permanent member of Nova. He doesn't have to perform or anything. Just walk around with his shirt off!"

Jisoo raised her hand. "I second!"

Min-ji still had her head buried in the pillow.

And me?

I was furious.

I scowled.

This wasn't over.

CHAPTER 23
LOGAN

A RUSTLING SOUND.

A soft sigh.

Then—

"Oh my—"

Voices.

Jisoo's? Loud. Shocked.

Then footsteps.

Something shifted against me, something warm.

My brain wasn't fully online yet, but I was already aware of three things:

1. Someone was pressed way too close to me.

2. I could feel fingers on my stomach. They were warm. Very nice.

3. The entire room was losing its damn mind.

I cracked one eye open.

Min-ji.

Pressed against my chest, her hand resting on my abs.

Jisoo gasped dramatically. "Oh. My. Giddy Aunt."

Then—more movement.

Min-ji's body stiffened against mine.

Her fingers twitched.

And then—

She launched herself off me so fast she nearly fell over the couch.

The next few minutes were hilarious. The banter between the girls was adorable and fun at the expense of a very embarrassed Min-ji.

After having a bit of fun, I sat up, stretching lazily, rolling my shoulders.

Hye-won grinned.

Min-ji refused to look at me, her entire face buried in the couch pillow.

Then Ji-an spoke.

"You," she said, voice clipped, "need to get dressed."

I blinked at her.

She was standing stiff, arms crossed, expression neutral.

Too neutral.

I glanced down at my ruined shirt, then back at her.

And then—just to be an asshole—I smirked.

"Min-ji, you're so bold," I said lazily, "I find that immensely attractive."

Min-ji's face may have been the most adorable thing I had ever seen. So freaking cute.

She let out a strangled squeak before collapsing face-first onto the couch.

Jisoo gasped dramatically, smacking my arm. "Shameless! Logan. You are so shameless!"

Hye-won was practically cackling. "You are the worst."

I was about to let it go, but then Ji-an clenched her jaw.

And I knew.

She was seething.

She was trying very hard not to show it.

And that?

That was interesting.

I pushed off the couch, stretching one last time before heading for the bathroom.

The second I shut the bathroom door behind me, I exhaled, gripping the edge of the sink.

Not because I was tired.

Not because I was sore.

But because, ONCE AGAIN, I needed a damn minute.

These women were going to be the death of me.

Too many pretty girls. Too compromising a situation. Too many moments that tested my patience and self-control. Geez. I was not used to this.

I turned the faucet on, letting the cold water run before splashing it over my face.

The chill helped.

Didn't fix everything, but it helped.

I stared at my reflection in the mirror, droplets rolling down my jaw.

I'd been in worse situations.

I'd been in far worse situations.

And yet, somehow, this—this cluster of an operation—was testing my patience more than it should have.

This night had been a mess.

The attack. The aftermath. The fact that I was still standing in a hotel suite with four beautiful women looking at me like I was some sort of savior.

It was complicated.

And Ji-an? What the hell was wrong with her?

I ran a hand down my face, exhaling as the memory hit me again. The one that kept me up most of the night.

Ji-an, straddling my lap.

Ji-an's fingers caressing my neck, my face, my mouth…

Ji-an, whispering in my ear.

Ji-an, asking, "Do you want to have sex with me?"

At that moment, I had wanted a few things in my life more than I wanted to rip Ji-an's clothes off and take her right there. The consequences be damned.

But then I realized, Ji-an… she wasn't random. She wasn't just a hookup. She was more than that. I didn't know her that well last night. I didn't know her any better this morning. But I knew that she wasn't someone who took intimacy lightly. It must have been her eyes that had given it away. One part lust, one part bad judgment. Another part, vulnerability and desire. Desire for what? I wasn't sure. Connection?

It was then that I understood.

The invite. I had been an impulse. A bold, poorly considered declaration. But most of all, it was a test.

She had wanted to see if I'd break. If I'd react the way every other man did around her.

I hadn't.

I'd touched her—just enough. Just to prove a point.

And then I asked her why.

She didn't have an answer.

Not a real one.

She'd leaned in, thinking she could turn the situation back in her favor—

And I had flicked her in the forehead.

I smirked slightly at the memory.

Because that?

That had driven her crazy.

She had stormed off, slammed the bedroom door, and left me with the knowledge that, for the first time in probably her life, someone had told her no.

I looked at my reflection and recalled how Ji-an looked after I flicked her. Considering my own actions, I realized it was sort of a dick move. But I figured if she was going to act ridiculous, then she couldn't be *too* upset when I hit her with some ridiculousness. Which is exactly what I did. Normally I would be more measured, but I figured she would have problems if I didn't make her understand. Flicking was the best way.

I sighed, wiping my face with a towel.

Ji-an was trouble, but I would have to deal with her later.

For now, I had to put that aside. I needed to get my shit together. I had a job to do, and it wasn't completed. Not yet.

The priority was getting Nova back to the Gorge.

They had another show tonight, and the last thing we needed was to disrupt their entire tour schedule. We were lucky that none of them got physically hurt last night and that the attack hadn't been announced to the entire world, which would have already put them behind. There was a lot of money riding on this tour, and people would not be happy if the schedule was interrupted. Delaying further would only create more problems—logistical, financial, and public relations nightmares that management wouldn't shut up about.

I was skeptical about them performing. As someone who had had their share of nightmares, it wasn't a good idea.

But it was above my pay grade, as much as it irked me.

For right now, we needed to move.

That meant handling three things immediately:

1. Personal security for each Nova member. No more lapses. No more chances. These girls weren't walking to the damn bathroom without someone watching them.

2. Coordinating statements for the police. The sooner we got this on record, the sooner we could control the narrative. We also needed a police presence at the Gorge.

3. Getting them on the road—safely. Get them into this show, perform their hearts out, and then get them on their way without any more incidents.

4. Find me a damn shirt. That one probably needed to be handled first.

The venue at the Gorge was already secured, but I'd have my team do another sweep. Double-check entry points, crowd management, and stage security. No one was getting anywhere near them without triple clearance, and they wouldn't be walking anywhere on those grounds without at least ten of my guys around.

It was time to call in some favors.

I exhaled sharply, gripping the sink.

And then my phone started vibrating again.

Emily.

I stared at the screen as it lit up, displaying the seventh missed call. Then the messages followed.

Emily (14 Unread Messages)

> Emily: Where the hell are you?
>
> Emily: Why aren't you answering?
>
> Emily: You were supposed to be home last night.
>
> Emily: Logan, pick up your damn phone.
>
> Emily: What's going on?
>
> Emily: Don't you dare ignore me.
>
> Emily: Brother of mine, you'd better be in a ditch somewhere, or when I find you, I am going to straight murder you! Call your sister!

I sighed, rubbing the back of my neck.

I didn't have time for this.

I shot back a single reply:

> Logan: Still working. The death match will need to come later. I need a favor.

Emily's response was immediate.

> Emily: A favor? Are you out of your
> fing mind? You disappear all night,
> don't answer me, and now you want a
> favor? I am seriously going to kill you!

I didn't bother explaining.

Logan: I need fresh clothes. Nova is heading back to the Gorge for their next show, but I need to change. Can you bring my stuff?

Three dots appeared.

Paused.

Then it disappeared.

Then reappeared.

> Emily: Fine. But you better have a
> damn good explanation when I get
> there, or be prepared for an ass-
> kicking.

I exhaled.

That was as much as I was going to get out of her right now.

I glanced down at my shirt—if you could even call it that anymore. It was torn, stretched, and completely unsalvageable.

I muttered a curse under my breath.

I hadn't packed extra. I wasn't supposed to be on the road with them—I was only meant to oversee the actual event venue, make sure everything ran smoothly.

That had changed fast.

I was in this now.

Which meant I needed to set the tone for how things were going to move forward.

They weren't going to like it.

Management was going to hate it.

But I wasn't running this show for their convenience.

I was running it for their safety. That meant getting these women out of this hotel and back to the Gorge before anyone realized just how serious this situation really was.

I exhaled, shaking off the last remnants of exhaustion.

Time to work.

I pushed open the bathroom door, stepping back into the suite—

And found Ji-an sitting on the edge of the couch, arms crossed, waiting for me. If looks could kill.

Well.

This was going to be fun.

CHAPTER 24
MIN-JI

THE MOMENT LOGAN VANISHED INTO THE BATHROOM, THE whispers exploded.

"Min-ji." Jisoo leaned in urgently, grabbing my arm like a detective cracking a major case. "You sneaky little fox."

I blinked, confused. "Wait—what did I do?"

Hye-won elbowed me playfully, eyes sparkling with mischief. "Don't play innocent. We saw the evidence. You were cuddling Logan like a satisfied bride the morning after her wedding!"

"I was not—"

She gestured dramatically to the couch. "Oh, really? Because his shirt didn't magically unbutton itself overnight."

I froze. That was true. That shirt Logan had torn from the fight was still on him. It was in bad shape, but it was still buttoned. How did it get unbuttoned?

I hadn't done that, right? My face burned hot as flashes of

memory surfaced—the warm skin, hard lines of muscle beneath my fingertips, my own embarrassing movement as I'd burrowed closer in my sleep.

Oh. My. Good. Lord.

Jisoo fanned herself theatrically. "Honestly, it was a whole drama scene. Like the heroine waking up in her handsome bodyguard's arms after some life-threatening incident. I am kind of pissed I didn't think of it."

"It wasn't like that," I hissed desperately, face flaming. "The last thing I remember is falling asleep in the car. I am totally innocent!"

"Your subconscious obviously wasn't," Hye-won teased. "It knew exactly what it wanted."

Jisoo nodded sagely. "Seriously. We applaud your bravery, Min-ji. None of us had the guts to make the first move."

Ji-an made an annoyed sound from her place on the edge of the couch. "No one made any moves. Stop being ridiculous."

"I don't know," Hye-won sighed dreamily. "I knew he was staying. I guess I didn't think about where he was going to sleep. Must have sat on the couch on the opposite side of Min-ji. The way I see it, sleeping next to Logan then snuggling up to him seems like a move to me. In fact, I call dibs tomorrow."

"You can't call dibs on Logan," I protested weakly.

Ji-an scowled. "That's not how dibs works."

"I'm pretty sure that's exactly how dibs works," Jisoo argued cheerfully. "Hye-won gets tomorrow, I get the day after. I won't sleep next to him though—that's too embarrassing. I'll settle for tracing his abs."

I gawked. "And that's not embarrassing? Are you joking?"

Jisoo shrugged. "You seemed to enjoy it."

"That is not an answer!" I almost yelled.

Ji-an let out a frustrated breath, rubbing her temples. "Do you hear yourselves right now? We trained at the agency surrounded by male idols, all of whom had amazing abs. Why are Logan's suddenly special?"

"Because they belong to Logan, who probably saved your lives last night," Jisoo said plainly, as if it were the most obvious thing in the world. "You don't have to participate if you don't appreciate fine art."

Ji-an glared at her. "You're both hopeless."

"Okay, fine." Hye-won raised her hand dramatically. "Ji-an is officially out of the Logan Appreciation Club."

Jisoo nodded solemnly. "Your loss, Ji-an."

Ji-an clenched her jaw, her frustration obvious even as she stayed quiet. But beneath the jokes, her annoyance felt real. My stomach knotted tightly. Hye-won and Jisoo were giggling and having fun, but Ji-an was genuinely irritated.

I swallowed nervously. "Look, I really didn't mean to do anything inappropriate. It just… happened."

Hye-won sighed wistfully, ignoring my obvious embarrassment. "Min-ji, you should just confess already. You've practically skipped five steps towards a relationship."

"What?" I squeaked. "I don't even know Logan!"

"Like that matters." Jisoo patted my shoulder with exaggerated sympathy. "He is handsome, brave, and stoic."

Ji-an's voice cut sharply through the teasing. "You should go back to your own room now. We need to get ready for the show tonight."

The chill in her voice wasn't subtle. I glanced at her, heart sinking at the rigid way she sat, arms crossed tightly, her expression carefully blank, yet clearly annoyed.

Jisoo and Hye-won might have been joking, but Ji-an wasn't.

She was pissed.

I stood quickly, followed by Jisoo and Hye-won, avoiding Ji-an's gaze. "Right. Um. I'll go get changed."

Ji-an didn't even glance up.

Grabbing my things hastily, I practically ran out of the suite, leaving laughter and whispers behind.

The hot water helped.

Or at least, it was supposed to help.

I stood under the steady stream, eyes closed, desperately hoping the heat would somehow wash away the burning embarrassment of this morning.

It didn't.

Because the couch incident wasn't even the worst of it. It wasn't what kept replaying in my mind, tormenting me on loop.

No, my mind was stuck on the moment Logan took me in his arms. Right after hurting those men.

Logan.

All I could see was his blue eyes.

Unlike Ji-an or Jisoo, I was Korean through and through. Born and raised just outside Seoul, pampered by a father who'd always indulged me more than he probably should have. Okay—so I was spoiled. I grew up binge-watching dramas like *Crash Landing on You*, *It's Okay Not to Be Okay*, and newer hits like *Love Next Door* and *Queen of Tears*, all of which had given me an unrealistic idea of romance.

But I'd always known it wasn't real.

Dramas are *meant* to be dramatic. People don't really fall accidentally into kisses. Girls don't actually stumble into danger, needing their love interest to catch them or save them from falling down stairs. Men and women don't stand two meters from each other and just stare for like ten minutes.

That is not a thing.

Those things simply don't happen in real life.

Handsome heroes don't appear out of nowhere to fight off attackers, saving the day at the very last second, risking death or grievous bodily harm. Women definitely don't rush into the arms of men they barely know after experiencing trauma. Men do not hold them tight and whisper warm words of strength and encouragement. Women don't cling to those men, desperate for comfort.

Women don't find themselves next to a handsome hero accidentally for warmth and safety.

Definitely not. That shit isn't real. Romance, love relationships, and even sex are messier, darker, and more practical.

But after the last twenty-four hours?

I probably needed to rethink my understanding of romance.

I closed my eyes tighter.

When those men appeared, spouting terrifying nonsense about Ji-an, I'd been scared—terrified in a way I'd never felt before. Sure, I'd had scary experiences—like that stalker from my trainee days—but police and management had handled that. It had felt controlled, distant.

This had been different. These men had knives, fanaticism burning in their eyes. I'd felt completely helpless, completely vulnerable, like the worst nightmares of my life had finally become real.

And then Logan appeared.

He'd brought violence. Brutal, overwhelming violence. Nothing I had ever seen in person. I'd watched him strike, dismantle those men with ruthless efficiency. He broke bones, dislocated joints, and crushed noses. He acted like a wrathful god. Terrifying. And yet, I'd felt no fear—not of him, at least. Only relief. Safety.

Now, standing here alone beneath the water of my shower in this hotel in a small town in another country, I could still feel the ghost of his arms around me. The memory of his steady voice whispering assurances into my hair:

You're safe. I won't let anything happen to you.

I squeezed my eyes shut, bracing my hands against the tile wall, my heartbeat erratic in my chest.

That experience had been enough to make my heart race.

And then this morning...

I'd woken up next to him.

Pressed close to his body, warmth radiating from his bare

skin, the steady rhythm of his heartbeat beneath my cheek. I remembered his words.

"How bold of you, Min-ji. I find that immensely attractive."

Those words brought a smile to my face.

I decided right there and then. It was time to learn more about Logan Cartner.

CHAPTER 25
EMILY

I PULLED INTO THE HOTEL PARKING LOT, CUTTING THE ENGINE with a sharp exhale.

Moses Lake wasn't exactly known for luxury accommodations, but this place? It wasn't bad. The penthouse level might have sounded impressive, but in a town of twenty-five thousand, it was just the top floor of a decent hotel. Nothing crazy.

Still, the sight of Logan's guys lingering near the entrance and parking lot made my stomach twist.

There were too many of them.

A cluster of men, all built like they lived in the gym, stood with the kind of alertness that screamed professional security. Their conversations were clipped, eyes sweeping the area, hands resting near their concealed holsters in that casual-but-ready way Logan always had when things were serious.

Something had happened.

Something big.

I already knew Logan wasn't telling me everything, but the way they looked at me as I walked past—silent nods, polite but firm—confirmed it.

This wasn't just work.

This was something else.

I swallowed, adjusting my grip on the duffel bag filled with Logan's fresh clothes. He hadn't packed extra, of course. Because God forbid he ever plan ahead.

The elevator ride felt longer than it should have, tension winding tight in my chest as I reached the penthouse floor.

I knocked on the door, shifting the weight of Logan's duffel in my grip, already half-annoyed before anyone even answered.

The hallway was quiet—too quiet. The kind of silence that made my skin prickle, like something had happened here that no one wanted to acknowledge.

I was about to knock again when the door cracked open.

And suddenly, I wasn't annoyed anymore.

Because holy shit.

The lead singer of Nova… Ji-an.

Standing there. Looking like she had just stepped out of a magazine cover.

I had seen pictures, videos, and blog posts of her, obviously. Everyone had. Ji-an of Nova—the kind of celebrity who wasn't just famous, but untouchable. The kind who walked into a room and made it feel like a stage.

But in person?

It wasn't fair.

She wasn't even dressed up—just an oversized, off-the-shoulder sweater, hanging loose against her collarbone, paired with simple leggings. But somehow, it made her look even better.

Like she had effortlessly woken up that beautiful. Like her hair, sleek and dark and falling perfectly around her face, hadn't been styled to perfection. Like her skin, smooth and glowing, wasn't the kind of flawless that made people question reality.

She wasn't wearing much makeup—just enough to make her features pop, her lips tinted a soft pink, her lashes long and curled.

I suddenly felt very aware of my own appearance.

My hoodie. My worn-out jeans. My definitely-not-done hair.

Yeah. This was bullshit. I am a huge freaking fan, and I come here looking like a homeless person.

I am going to kill my brother.

Ji-an smiled, and it was the kind of smile that should have been illegal—soft, warm, with just the faintest hint of amusement.

"You must be Emily," she said. "You're just as pretty as Logan described you."

Her voice was low, smooth. The kind of voice that made you lean in just to hear more of it.

I blinked, momentarily disarmed. "Uh. Yeah."

She knew my name?

She stepped aside, motioning me in. "Logan's inside."

I hesitated for a fraction of a second before stepping through the door.

The suite was nice. Not over-the-top luxury, but expensive enough. Comfortable enough. Lived-in enough.

Which was the part that caught me off guard.

There were clothes draped over the chairs. A half-empty coffee cup on the table. The lingering scent of something warm—coffee and vanilla.

And my brother?

This wasn't just a meeting space.

They had stayed here.

Together.

And just as that realization was starting to sink in—

The bathroom door swung open.

And Logan stepped out.

Wearing nothing but a towel.

"Em, is that you?"

I nearly dropped the bag.

"What. The. Hell," I snapped, my voice sharper than I intended. "You better start talking, Logan."

Ji-an immediately turned away, her arms tightening around herself, her head ducking slightly like she physically couldn't look at him.

Logan sighed, running a hand through his damp hair.

"This isn't what it looks like," he said.

I let out a sharp, humorless laugh. "Oh, really? Because it looks like you spent the night in a hotel with an international superstar and now you're walking around half-naked while she refuses to even glance in your direction. He didn't do anything to you, did he Ji-an? Because I will kick his ass if he did!"

Ji-an's jaw tightened.

She definitely wasn't looking at him. I had been half-joking. Did my brother really hook up with the lead singer of Nova?

Oh.

Oh, this was interesting.

I crossed my arms. "Well?"

Logan exhaled slowly. "I'll explain everything. Give me a moment."

"You better," I said, my tone cutting.

Because whatever this was?

It was a lot.

I gestured wildly between him and Ji-an.

Neither of them said anything.

Which only made it worse.

I took a slow step forward, lowering my voice. "Did something happen?"

Something flickered across Logan's expression—too fast to catch, but there.

Ji-an's arms tightened around herself.

Oh yeah. Something had happened.

And I wasn't leaving until I found out exactly what it was.

Logan nodded and went into the bathroom.

CHAPTER 26
JI-AN

LOGAN WENT TO CHANGE, LEAVING ME ALONE WITH HIS SISTER.

Emily was here.

I took a deep breath, trying to steady the rapid beat of my heart. It was strange seeing her in person. We'd spent countless late nights chatting online—Emily sharing her worries, me comforting her as Jess—but she had absolutely no idea she'd been talking to Ji-an, the leader of Nova.

She smiled nervously, eyes wide. "So… hi. You're actually Ji-an."

"Guilty," I said lightly. "And you're Emily. Logan's sister, right?"

Emily's cheeks turned pink instantly. "Yeah. Wait, how do you—?"

She stopped, shaking her head with embarrassment. "Dumb question. Logan probably mentioned me. Sorry, I'm just… a bit starstruck."

I laughed softly, immediately charmed. "Actually, I've seen your modeling on Instagram. You're really talented."

Her eyes widened, and panic flashed briefly over her face. "Wait—you've seen my modeling? Oh good lord, did Logan—?"

I shook my head quickly. "Relax, Logan only mentioned he had a pretty little sister who modeled. But I recognized your name when he said it. Your feed is gorgeous—especially the Newtown skincare shoot."

Emily's face turned a deeper shade of red. "You've actually seen my Instagram…"

I smiled, gently amused. "Yes. You're stunning, Emily. Your work caught my attention."

She exhaled shakily, laughing nervously. "Wow. I'm sorry, it's just… surreal. Ji-an from Nova looking at my stuff and calling me gorgeous? I feel like I'm hallucinating. You're literally perfect in person."

"Well, thank you." I ducked my head slightly, genuinely touched. "But don't sell yourself short. You're incredible."

Emily's phone buzzed, and she glanced down quickly, typing a fast response. "Sorry—my boyfriend," she explained with a shy smile. "He's a little clingy."

I tilted my head, intrigued. "Ahh, that can be cute. Are you two serious?"

She shook her head quickly. "Not really. It's still new. My last relationship was… bad. He treated me terribly. When Logan found out, he went ballistic. Pretty sure my ex is still running."

I smiled knowingly. "I understand. My last boyfriend was a disaster."

Emily's eyes widened instantly. "Oh—right. Sorry. Everyone knows about that."

I grimaced. "Unfortunately. But honestly, I should've known better. I wasn't that into him, and he was way too into me. That's always a recipe for disaster. Especially male K-pop idols. They cannot handle the blow to their egos."

She softened, giving me a sympathetic look. "Truth. Well, I hope you find someone better."

I grinned playfully. "Know anyone?"

Emily laughed, startled. "I could set you up! Can you imagine if I hooked you up with one of my college friends? Heads would explode."

"Exactly what I need," I joked. "Mass scandal. I can already see the headlines."

Emily straightened, mimicking a news anchor. "Ji-an from Nova Causes Mass Casualties on Blind Date Night—Story at 11."

We both burst out laughing, and a loud snort escaped from me.

Emily's eyes lit up. "Good lord, you're adorable."

"Stop," I protested, covering my mouth. "You're making me blush."

Logan reappeared from the bedroom, fully dressed, sliding his phone into his pocket. "Sorry. Had to update the police."

Emily's expression shifted instantly, concerned. "Logan, seriously, what happened last night?"

Logan sighed, expression sobering. "It was an organized attack. Fanatics obsessed with Ji-an. They had knives. It got ugly fast."

Emily's eyes widened. "Are you guys okay?"

"Yeah," Logan reassured her, glancing at me briefly. "Everyone's mostly fine. The agency, management, and local authorities are on edge, though. We're moving Nova back to the Gorge for the second show."

I swallowed, warmth flooding my chest as he glanced my way. "We're safe because of Logan. Honestly, if he hadn't intervened, we might be dead. There were like ten guys."

Emily shot to her feet, horrified. "You fought ten people? Logan, that's insane—"

"Wait," Logan interrupted quickly, holding up his hands. "Five. It was five, not ten—I'm not a superhero."

"Five's not much better," I pointed out, shaking my head.

Emily folded her arms tightly. "Seriously, Logan? Five?"

Logan just shrugged uncomfortably. "It's my job."

His phone buzzed again, and he glanced down, sighing. "I have to take this—it's Sonya." He stepped out again, leaving us alone.

I blinked.

Sonya? Who the hell is Sonya? And why would Logan interrupt this for her?

Emily exhaled, visibly relaxing now that Logan had stepped out. "Sorry about him. He's... a lot."

"Yeah," I muttered, distracted. "I've noticed."

She glanced at me apologetically. "If Logan's been difficult—"

"Excuse me?" Logan's voice echoed back from the other room. "Why are you assuming I caused problems? Ji-an, maybe tell Emily how you tried to seduce me."

"WHAT?" Emily and I shouted simultaneously.

"Oh, don't be shy," Logan called, clearly enjoying himself. "It's a funny story."

My face burned. "I'm going to kill him," I whispered fiercely.

Just then, the suite door burst open, and Jisoo, Min-ji, and Hye-won stumbled in, chattering loudly until they noticed Emily.

"Oh," Jisoo blinked, curious but confused. "Hi. Who are you?"

Emily stood nervously. "Oh. Wow. Yeah. Of course. The rest of Nova. I should have thought of that. Um, hi! I'm Emily. Logan's sister."

All three girls froze, eyes wide.

Min-ji gasped dramatically. "Logan has a sister? And you're her? Oh my—hi!"

Hye-won squealed excitedly. "You're Logan's sister? We have so many questions!"

Jisoo leaned forward eagerly. "Has he always looked like that? Was he always so—"

"Hot?" Hye-won supplied helpfully.

Emily flushed crimson. "Um, he's my brother, so…"

"Right. Awkward," Jisoo conceded quickly. "But does he have a girlfriend?"

Emily laughed awkwardly, glancing briefly toward me. "No girlfriend. Logan's… not really a relationship guy."

Min-ji leaned forward, shy but insistent. "Really? He's single?"

Emily nodded hesitantly. "As far as I know."

Min-ji blushed fiercely. "Does he have a type? Like, does he prefer cute girls or sexy ones?"

Emily looked overwhelmed but thoughtful. "Honestly, Logan's dated all sorts. Tall, blonde, busty girls. A Japanese exchange student in high school. A half-Indian girl in college. He has a childhood friend or two out there. But none of them lasted. Since starting his security firm, he's been all work and no play."

"Boring," Hye-won sighed dramatically.

"Guys, seriously," I groaned, rolling my eyes. "Ease up."

Jisoo smirked knowingly at me. "Don't pretend you're not interested too, Ji-an."

Emily's eyes widened mischievously. "Wait, so you actually did try to seduce him?"

Her voice was playful, but the damage was immediate.

All three members of Nova froze, staring at me with open mouths. The silence was deafening.

Just then, Logan walked by, glancing in casually. "Em, don't cause rumors. I was joking. Obviously, Ji-an's out of my league. Girls, I need you downstairs in half an hour. Your security team is expecting us within the hour." He left before I could respond.

Min-ji gasped dramatically. "Ji-an, you and Logan?"

I buried my face in my hands. "Don't even start."

Emily laughed apologetically. "Sorry. Logan's kind of stupid around normal women, let alone famous ones."

Min-ji huffed, crossing her arms. "I don't know, I think he's pretty smooth. He should really be doing something else, though. His face is totally wasted in security. He's practically a walking K-drama lead."

Emily laughed softly. "You know what? You're not wrong."

I nudged Emily excitedly. "Enough Logan talk. You have a boyfriend? And he's clingy?"

Emily blushed brightly. "Yeah, he is. Honestly, it's embarrassing how much he worries."

"Ugh, jealous," Jisoo sighed dramatically.

Emily's phone buzzed again, and she rolled her eyes affectionately. "See? He never stops."

I smiled, watching the easy banter between them. Emily relaxed, the awkwardness finally fading.

Logan leaned in from the doorway, eyeing us suspiciously. "Did something happen?"

Emily grinned sweetly. "Just girl talk. Your favorite."

He sighed dramatically. "Fantastic."

His eyes met mine for a heartbeat, warmth fluttering in my chest. He frowned slightly, clearly sensing something, but he let it go.

And for now, I wanted to keep it exactly that way.

CHAPTER 27
JI-AN

I was in a better mood by the time we went downstairs. Emily was exactly like I thought she would be. Some people are very different from their online persona, myself included, but Emily was who she was, and she didn't act like anything else. It was awesome.

So I was in a really good mood, even with last night's drama and Min-ji's attempt to get ahead of me. I was in a good mood—until she showed up.

Tall. Slender. Russian or Eastern European. Not movie-star gorgeous, but effortlessly striking. Dark blonde hair, high cheekbones, a slight scar across her cheek, sharp blue eyes that immediately locked onto Logan.

She walked toward him, the sort of long-legged, shapely walk that runway models use. People watched as this woman walked. She was tall.

I am pretty tall too, just not like her. My eyes wandered around her. It's not like she was making ME insecure, but damn, was she beautiful. I couldn't help but wonder if Logan thought so too. She wore a business suit, something you'd probably see on Wall Street, except she had a gun on her hip. It was like she was some sort of sexy spy.

I will never get used to the open carry rules in the U.S. Don't get me wrong, I love it. But it's still a little unsettling compared to Korea or Australia.

Her eyes were a deep hazel color, and her lips curled slightly as she approached. "Carter."

Logan exhaled. "Sonya. Glad you could make it."

I froze.

Jisoo grabbed my arm.

Hye-won's eyes widened. "Oh no."

Sonya crossed her arms, her smirk deepening. "Didn't think you'd be the one making headlines."

Logan ran a hand down his face. "Please don't start."

She laughed.

Like they had some kind of inside joke.

Like they had history.

And suddenly, I hated her.

I didn't even know why.

"Who is she?" I muttered to Min-ji.

Min-ji, still recovering from her own embarrassment, peeked over. "How should I know?"

Emily actually spoke up. "Freelancer. Security computer specialist. She's not on Logan's team, but… she works with him a lot."

Jisoo muttered, "Oh, this is bad."

Hye-won smirked. "You're mad."

"I am not mad."

"You so are."

"I don't care."

Hye-won grinned. "Right. That's why you're glaring at her like she personally offended your bloodline."

I was not glaring. I was assessing the situation.

And the situation was that I did not like the way this woman looked at Logan.

Sonya tilted her head, giving me a once-over.

Then she smirked.

Like she knew something I didn't.

And I snapped.

I turned to Logan, forcing my sweetest smile. "We're leaving. Now."

Logan blinked. "We are?"

"Yes."

Sonya raised an eyebrow, clearly amused.

But Logan?

Logan sighed. "Looks like I've been summoned."

"Looks like," Sonya murmured, eyes flicking between us. "I will meet you at the venue. We have much to discuss. You owe me big time, and I intend to collect."

I turned on my heel, walking away before I did something really stupid.

And Logan, after a beat, followed.

CHAPTER 28
LOGAN

THE SECURITY OFFICE WAS CHAOTIC.

The moment Sonya and I stepped inside, a sharp bite filled the air, punctuated by the unmistakable authority of a man used to being obeyed.

A man in a navy suit stood at the center of the room, *furious*, barking at the security team in rapid-fire Korean.

Lee Jae-won.

CEO of Hwa International, the parent company of JP Medi —the corporation that owned Nova.

Lee Min-hyuk's father.

I'd met a lot of powerful men in my life, and Lee Jae-won fit the mold perfectly. Sharp-eyed, composed, dangerous in the way only businessmen who controlled entire industries could be. His voice cut through the room, demanding answers, his security team barely able to stammer out responses under his scrutiny.

I recognized the type.

A man who expected control. Who did not tolerate failure. Who could end someone's career with a single phone call.

But when he turned and saw me—his entire demeanor shifted.

His anger didn't vanish, but it refocused. Sharpened.

His gaze locked onto me, cool and unreadable, and then—to my surprise—he inclined his head slightly.

"Mr. Carter."

His tone was polite. Controlled.

I nodded back. "Mr. Lee."

"You have my gratitude for what you did last night," he continued, voice smooth. "Nova is a global treasure, and if anything had happened to them…" His lips pressed into a thin line. "I would not have been pleased."

There was something weighty about the way he said it. A promise. Or a warning.

"Just doing my job," I said evenly.

His lips twitched slightly. Not quite a smile. "Perhaps. But you still have my thanks."

Sonya, leaning casually against a desk, let out a quiet scoff. She wasn't even trying to hide her amusement, watching the exchange like it was a particularly entertaining drama.

Lee Jae-won turned back to his security team, snapping something in Korean. They practically bolted from the room.

When the door shut behind them, it left only the three of us.

He exhaled slowly, adjusting his cufflinks. "I assume you are here to discuss security measures for tonight's event."

"I am," I said. "But I also want to talk about something else."

His brow lifted slightly. "Oh?"

"The Brotherhood."

Sonya stiffened next to me.

I didn't blame her. This wasn't exactly something I had planned on saying. Not yet.

But the moment I said it, I knew I had his attention.

Lee Jae-won went still.

Then, after a beat, he let out a quiet breath. "Interesting," he murmured. "And what, exactly, do you want to know about them?"

Sonya shot me a look, one that practically screamed, *What the hell are you doing?*

But I ignored her.

Because the way he reacted—calm, knowing—told me exactly what I needed to know.

He wasn't surprised by the name.

He already knew.

I crossed my arms. "First, let's discuss the breach."

He studied me for a moment, then gave a small nod. "Very well. What do you need to know?"

"The attackers last night were organized," I said. "This wasn't just a handful of obsessed fans. Their movements were coordinated. Their goal was clear." I exhaled. "And they almost succeeded."

Lee Jae-won's expression didn't change, but something in his posture shifted.

"You think there is a larger network at play."

"I know there is," I corrected.

His jaw tightened. "I was assured that security at the venue was adequate. Yet somehow, this… The Brotherhood was able to bypass it." His voice was measured, but there was steel underneath. "That is unacceptable."

"It wasn't just a lapse in security," I said. "It was a planned infiltration. Your team got outmaneuvered."

A muscle in his jaw twitched.

I wasn't just talking to a CEO—I was talking to a man who had built an empire. He wasn't used to being told his systems had weaknesses.

But he didn't argue.

Instead, he turned his head slightly. "Min-hyuk."

A fourth voice joined the conversation.

I turned.

Lee Min-hyuk entered. Unlike his father, his expression wasn't unreadable. It was tight. Frustrated.

And maybe… embarrassed.

I hadn't even realized he was here. He had been silent while his father handled the yelling, but now that the conversation had shifted, he stepped forward.

"My team is already reviewing the breach," he said. His voice was controlled, but there was something behind it—like he was forcing himself to sound professional. "We're pulling surveillance, analyzing access logs, reviewing communications from last week."

Sonya arched an eyebrow. "And? What have you found?"

Min-hyuk hesitated, glancing at his father.

Lee Jae-won nodded once. "Speak freely."

Min-hyuk exhaled sharply. "The attackers weren't using fake credentials. They bypassed security completely. No forged IDs. No access passes. They moved like they knew the weak points in the system."

Sonya's eyes flickered. "An inside job?"

Min-hyuk frowned. "Possibly. Or someone who had prior knowledge of the venue's security layout."

Lee Jae-won's expression darkened. "Unacceptable."

I nodded. "Which brings us to the other reason I'm here." I motioned toward Sonya. "I brought in extra help. Sonya, don't bother asking for a last name; she won't give you one. She is running her own investigation into the Brotherhood's online activity at my request."

Lee Jae-won's gaze flicked to her, sharp and assessing.

She didn't flinch. Just smirked. "Nice to meet you."

He nodded once. "And what have you found?"

Sonya pulled out her phone, tapping through a few screens before holding it up. "Most of the Brotherhood's online activity is funneling to two major locations: Northern California." She tapped again. "And Seoul."

Lee Jae-won nodded for her to continue.

Sonya continued her narration. "This group is way more well-funded than some online Red-pill frat should be. There are retreats, recruiting, and fundraisers. There is even a request for tax exemption under a religious 503(c)(3). This group has an agenda. It's unlikely they are going to stop after this attack."

The room went silent.

Then—

Lee Jae-won exhaled, closing his eyes briefly. Like he had just confirmed something he didn't want to be true. "That's what I was afraid of."

I narrowed my eyes. "You knew."

He nodded. "This isn't the first time we've had fanatics go crazy. This seems like an extra bit of insane and a little too organized. So, like you, Mr. Carter, I had some people check into things. We found much of what Ms. Sonya has stated, but not really as well detailed."

Sonya and I exchanged glances but didn't say anything.

He glanced at his phone. "They are more than your typical group. The mere fact that they were able to injure Si-woo is testament to that. Thank you for saving him as well, Mr. Carter. He says that he owes you a bottle of Soju."

I laughed. "Never drank the stuff."

Mr. Lee gave a rare smile.

CHAPTER 29
LOGAN

Lee Jae-won was quiet for a long moment. Considering. Weighing something in his mind.

I knew men like him. Men who didn't make decisions lightly. Who saw the world in terms of risks and rewards.

Finally, he exhaled. "Do you trust her?"

He meant Sonya.

I didn't hesitate. "She's the best at what she does."

Sonya's lips curled slightly, but she didn't say anything. Just watched, waiting.

Lee Jae-won glanced at her again, studying her with that same unreadable expression. Then, after a beat, he gave a single nod.

"Ms. Sonya, I would like to hire you," he said.

She grinned. "Are you sure? I am really expensive."

Mr. Lee snorted. "I will pay triple your rate. Email your account details here."

He handed her his business card.

"I will expect updates on anything you uncover. This Brotherhood is a real threat. I want to find and crush them. I want to know everything."

Sonya tilted her head. "You got it, boss man."

Min-hyuk looked like he was barely holding back an eye roll.

His father ignored the flippant tone, already turning back toward his desk. "I will have my team coordinate with you." He looked at me. "And I expect this will remain discreet."

I nodded. "That's the plan."

Lee Jae-won's gaze lingered for a moment longer, then he motioned toward his son. "Min-hyuk, escort them out. I need to make some calls."

We exited the room as Mr. Lee's advisors closed in.

Min-hyuk's expression twisted in irritation, his jaw tightening. "You people are a joke. How ridiculous."

Sonya didn't even bother looking at him. "Keeping the girls safe? Yeah, how ridiculous."

His eyes snapped to me, sharp and full of resentment. "We don't need her poking around in our business. And we sure as hell don't need some foreigner taking control of security like he owns the place."

I exhaled through my nose. "I am in charge of security. This is my backyard, not yours. You're guests here, not the other way around."

His face darkened.

I held his gaze, my voice even. "Your security protocols failed. My guys checked. The perimeter security? Fine. No issues. The threat didn't come from the crowd, didn't come from any of the regular checkpoints. It came from inside— from your VIP area. The one managed exclusively by your people." I stepped forward, lowering my voice just enough to make sure he understood. "And one of them was directly tied to a group making threats against Ji-an."

Min-hyuk scoffed. "That's impossible. Haw Si-woo would never allow that."

"You damn right he wouldn't," I growled. "But Han wasn't the one overseeing; he was with Nova. It was one of his subordinates who fed up so royally."

He glared at me, then at Sonya.

Sonya, completely unbothered, just smirked. "It's cute how much denial you've got going on."

Min-hyuk's fists clenched. "I don't have to stand here and listen to this."

I nodded once. "No, you don't."

His jaw tightened further, his body practically vibrating with restrained frustration. But he wasn't going to win this argument.

He knew it.

So, like a spoiled rich kid who didn't get his way, he turned and stormed out of the security office, slamming the door behind him.

The second he was gone, Sonya let out a low whistle. "What a clown. All that money wasted on an idiot."

I sighed, rubbing the bridge of my nose. "He'll get over it."

She shrugged. "Or he won't. Either way, it's not our problem."

"What can you tell me about those two hubs?" I asked as Min-hyuk walked away.

She shrugged. "Could be a hub, could be a base. Either way, it's worth looking into. I'll keep you updated."

I nodded. "Good. You really are the best."

She smirked. "Aw, was that a compliment?"

I exhaled sharply. "Don't start."

Sonya stepped in closer, her sharp blue eyes locking onto mine. "What, you don't want to tell me how grateful you are?"

I shook my head, already knowing where this was going.

Didn't stop her, though.

She reached up, fingers curling into the front of my vest, and pulled me in.

Her lips crashed into mine, firm, confident, and teasing all at once.

Sonya had always done this.

Always tested boundaries. Always played her little games.

And I'd always tolerated it.

Because who didn't like being kissed by a striking woman?

But this time—

This time, it was different.

She didn't just kiss me. She deepened it.

She tilted her head, pressing in harder, her fingers tightening against my chest.

She was playing with me as always.

Seeing if I'd let her push further.

For half a second, I almost did.

Almost let myself sink into it, let myself forget that I was standing in a security office, that I was still on duty, that I had an entire venue to lock down. And Sonya wasn't actually my type.

Then, just as quickly, I pulled back.

She smiled against my lips, letting me go just as easily as she had grabbed me. "Still got it."

I exhaled, adjusting my vest. "Sonya."

She winked. "Don't get all worked up, Captain. Just wanted to remind you what you're missing."

I snorted. "What am I missing? The last time I checked, you were into girls."

She cocked an eyebrow. "What does that have to do with it?"

"It's obvious what it means," I said. "I am not a girl."

Sonya just grinned. "I will always make an exception for you, Logan, you know that."

I sighed and pinched the bridge of my nose. "Never mind. Try not to get yourself killed."

She tapped my chest lightly, stepping back. "You, too."

Then she turned and walked off, hips swaying, confidence radiating from every step.

I ran a hand down my face.

I didn't have time for this.

I straightened, already shifting gears.

This show was going to go off without a hitch.

No more mistakes.

No more breaches.

Then Nova would go off to the next venue, and they were no longer my problem.

Yeah, right.

CHAPTER 30
JI-AN

THE CROWD WAS ELECTRIC.

A sea of flashing lightsticks, glowing pink and silver, waved in perfect rhythm with the beat of our music. Thousands of voices called our names, some chanting in sync, others screaming whatever they could just to be heard.

I had performed in massive venues before, but every time, it still hit me like the first.

That raw, overwhelming energy.

That instant when the entire world blurred into a single, breathless moment.

And this was our moment.

As the final notes of the last song faded, Min-ji, Hye-won, Jisoo, and I gathered at the front of the stage, catching our breath.

The audience roared louder, and I lifted the mic, grinning as I called out in Korean, "Moses Lake, how are you feeling?!"

The crowd erupted.

Someone near the front screamed, "I LOVE YOU, JI-AN!"

Another voice cut through the noise, "WILL YOU MARRY ME?!"

I laughed, shaking my head. "Marriage? Already? You move fast!"

Hye-won turned to me, mic still in hand. "Hey, Ji-an, should we get a group wedding? Since apparently, they want to marry all of us!"

Min-ji wiped the sweat from her forehead dramatically. "That's too many husbands! I think I'd rather just stay single!"

The crowd exploded with laughter and cheers.

Jisoo smirked, flipping her hair back. "I don't know, I kind of like the idea of a stadium full of people competing for my hand."

The audience lost it.

Min-ji clutched her chest, pretending to swoon. "Jisoo is too powerful. I can't compete!"

The fans screamed even louder, chanting Jisoo's name like they were declaring war.

I grinned, looking out at them all.

This.

This was why I loved what we did.

The connection. The joy. The way we could make people forget everything else for just a little while.

Min-ji took a deep breath, wiping at her eyes. "You guys really are amazing. Every time we perform, we feel so lucky."

Hye-won nodded. "We're so grateful for each and every one of you. Thank you for loving us."

The fans cheered, waving their banners, some holding up signs with our names, some crying, some just beaming.

Jisoo turned to me, her eyes gleaming mischievously. "Ji-an, don't you have something to say to them?"

I smirked, playing along. "Of course." I raised my mic again, looking out at the thousands of faces.

"Moses Lake, WE LOVE YOU!!"

The screams were so loud they shook the floor.

It felt perfect.

Until it wasn't.

———

The moment came out of nowhere.

One second, we were still laughing, still thriving in the energy.

The next—

My chest locked up.

The lights were too bright. The crowd was too loud. The stage felt too big.

My breath hitched.

My vision blurred at the edges.

And suddenly, I couldn't hear the music anymore.

I could only hear my own heartbeat, hammering against my ribs.

No, no, no.

Not now.

I gripped the mic tighter, focusing on the weight of it in my hand, grounding myself.

But my hands felt unsteady.

I was fine. I had been fine—

And then, I saw them.

A few men, standing near the back of the venue.

They weren't doing anything. Weren't holding signs, weren't dancing like the rest of the crowd.

They were just watching.

Something about them sent a chill up my spine.

The Brotherhood was gone. Logan had handled it. Security was tight. There was no way they could be here.

No way. But my body didn't care about logic. Fear curled at the edges of my thoughts, creeping in.

I took a step back—

And then, past the lights, past the blur of movement—

I saw him.

Standing just off to the side.

Watching.

Steady.

Logan.

Arms crossed, scanning the crowd, sharp, focused, calm.

Like always.

Like he wasn't going to let anything happen to us.

And just like that—

I could breathe again.

The pressure in my chest loosened. The moment snapped, like something breaking free inside of me.

I pulled in a breath, forced my body to move—one step,

then another—until I was dancing again, until I was singing again, until the music drowned out everything else.

Until I was back in control.

The panic passed.

The fear faded.

And the show went on.

———

By the time we hit the final bow, I was exhausted.

But happy.

The moment we stepped offstage, the adrenaline crashed.

Min-ji practically collapsed onto me, still giggling. Hye-won fanned herself dramatically. Jisoo was wiping sweat from her face, her usual composure cracked just enough for me to know she was just as drained as the rest of us.

Then—

Mr. Lee, the CEO of StarRise Entertainment, stepped forward, still beaming.

"You girls were incredible tonight," he praised, clapping his hands together. "You continue to prove why Nova is the best in the industry."

Min-hyuk stood beside him, stiff and unreadable.

The smile on Mr. Lee's face widened as he handed each of us a bouquet of flowers, the scent of fresh roses filling the air.

"You all deserve this. Truly."

I bowed politely, accepting the flowers, but…

Something felt off.

I glanced at Min-hyuk.

He barely looked at us.

He was standing there, next to his father, going through the motions. Saying nothing.

And yet, every time he did look at us—

It was like his mind was somewhere else.

I could tell Min-ji and Hye-won noticed it too, but none of us said anything.

Not yet.

Because then, Logan stepped forward.

And just like that—

We felt better.

He was still in his black tactical gear, still radiating that sharp, no-nonsense presence that made it impossible to ignore him.

His eyes flickered over us, scanning, checking.

It was the same look he had given me on stage.

The one that had pulled me back from the edge.

I met his gaze.

Didn't say anything.

Didn't need to.

He nodded. Just slightly.

And that was enough.

We were safe.

We had made it.

CHAPTER 31
LOGAN

THE SECURITY OFFICE AT THE VENUE WAS QUIETER NOW, THE chaos of the night finally winding down. The concert had gone off without a hitch, Nova was safely backstage, and the fans were starting to clear out.

I should have felt relieved.

But I wasn't done yet.

I stood near the window, arms crossed, my focus still locked on the night outside. The adrenaline had faded, but my mind was still running through every possible angle.

The Brotherhood was still out there.

And I wasn't leaving without getting some answers.

The door behind me opened.

I turned just as Lee Jung-hwan, CEO of JP Media, stepped inside, flanked by a few of his executives and his son, Lee Min-hyuk.

Min-hyuk looked as smug as ever, though there was

something in his expression—a simmering irritation, barely contained. Like he'd rather be anywhere but here.

I didn't bother acknowledging him.

Instead, I turned to Lee Jung-hwan.

"Is Han Si-woo alright?" I asked.

Lee's gaze sharpened. "He's stable. He was taken to a private facility for treatment. It'll take time, but he'll recover."

Good. Si-woo was a professional, and his absence would be felt. But at least he was still breathing.

Lee's attention shifted, and I followed his gaze to the envelope sitting on the table.

He picked it up, turned toward me, and extended it. "This is for you."

I didn't take it immediately. Instead, I met his gaze.

"You already have a contract with Archangel Protective Services," I said evenly. "This wasn't part of the deal."

"This isn't for your company." His voice was firm. "It's for you—a personal thank-you for ensuring Nova's safety."

Min-hyuk scoffed. "It's absurd. He was just doing his job."

Lee didn't even glance at him.

I let the silence stretch, then finally reached out and took the envelope.

It was heavy.

A hell of a lot more than I expected.

I didn't count it, but I didn't have to. I had enough experience to know this was life-changing money.

Lee watched me carefully. "This isn't a bribe, Mr. Carter."

I nodded. "I didn't think it was."

"It's an acknowledgment," he continued. "You saw what happened tonight. You saw how close we came to disaster. Nova is one of JP Media's greatest assets. I take their security very seriously."

Min-hyuk let out a laugh, shaking his head. "And yet, it was his security that failed. If you'd had better people from the start, this wouldn't have happened."

I turned to him slowly.

Min-hyuk met my gaze, smug and entitled.

"I was in charge of venue security," I said, my voice measured. "Nova's personal security was your responsibility."

His smug expression faltered, just slightly.

Lee didn't say anything, but I could tell he wasn't impressed with his son's attitude either.

I shifted gears. "You saw the footage," I said to Lee. "So tell me—what do you know about the Brotherhood?"

That got his attention.

Min-hyuk stiffened slightly, but Lee remained still, watching me with calculated interest.

"What makes you think I know anything?" he asked.

I held his gaze. "Because you've been in this industry long enough to know what happens behind the curtain. You knew the moment you saw that footage that this wasn't just an isolated incident."

He exhaled slowly, and for the first time, I saw it—the flicker of something behind his eyes.

Recognition.

Understanding.

And just a little bit of concern.

"The Brotherhood isn't just a cult," he admitted. "They have money. Influence. They're organized."

Min-hyuk scoffed. "It's an online conspiracy. Some fringe group of losers playing vigilante."

Lee shot him a sharp look. "Do you think what happened last night was nothing?"

Min-hyuk didn't answer.

Lee exhaled. "Fanatics or not, they were able to penetrate our security, take down trained special forces, and based on what I saw, they fully intended to take Ji-an and hurt the others."

I nodded. "The cops are already involved here in the US. It's probably time to get the Korean authorities involved as well."

Mr. Lee considered this, then nodded his head in approval.

At that moment, my phone buzzed.

I pulled it out, glancing at the screen.

Sonya: *New lead. Brotherhood's Seoul operations linked to a building owned by Chairman Kang of Apex Holdings. Call me.*

My grip tightened slightly around the phone.

Apex Holdings. Another one of those massive Korean conglomerates.

I looked up, meeting his gaze. "Have you ever done business with Chairman Kang?"

Lee's jaw tightened. "We move in the same circles, but no. I wouldn't trust him as far as I could throw him."

"Well," I said, slipping my phone back into my pocket. "Looks like the Brotherhood is operating out of one of his buildings."

Lee went still.

Min-hyuk frowned. "What?"

I nodded. "That's what I was just told. His company either owns it directly, or one of his subsidiaries does. Either way, it's a connection."

Lee muttered something under his breath, rubbing his temple. "This is bad."

Min-hyuk's frown deepened. "This is bullshit. Some foreigner sends a text, and you just take it as fact? We should have our people looking into this—not trusting some outsider."

I barely held back an eye roll.

Lee shot him a warning look. "Your attitude is unnecessary."

Min-hyuk scoffed, shoving away from the table. "This is a waste of time."

Then, without another word, he turned and stormed out.

I exhaled, shaking my head. "He's a real piece of work."

Lee sighed. "That's putting it mildly."

I refocused. "If we're going to keep Nova safe, we need more information. You should stay in touch with Sonya. She's the best at what she does."

Lee studied me for a moment, then nodded. "Understood."

I nodded back, slipping the envelope into my vest.

This was far from over.

But right now?

I had one last job tonight.

Make sure the rest of this night went off without a hitch.

CHAPTER 32
LOGAN

THE MOMENT I STEPPED INTO THE DRESSING ROOM, I KNEW something was off.

Not because the lights were dimmed or because the air smelled like lingering perfume and hairspray. Not because the room was too quiet—too expectant.

No.

I knew something was off because Hye-won was smirking.

And in my experience, nothing good ever came from an expression like that.

The door clicked shut behind me. My eyes flicked over the room in a quick, automatic sweep. Jisoo and Hye-won were draped over the couch in various states of undress. I wouldn't say they were imitating wear or anything, but there was way more skin than I should be seeing.

One would expect the girls to be upset, cover up, scream out that I was a pervert, do something. But nothing of the sort happened. Jisoo's face was a bit red but otherwise smiling. Hye-won was completely casual. Completely deliberate.

She just grinned like a shark, and of course, she was showing the most skin.

Ji-an was by the vanity, pretending she wasn't involved, and maybe she wasn't, as she was way more covered up than Jisoo or Hye-won. Her head was turned slightly, looking at her reflection, like she just happened to be standing there in a cropped top and shorts.

And Min-ji?

Min-ji looked like she wanted to die.

The youngest member of Nova was standing stiffly by the clothing rack and was mostly dressed, but still, her face was bright red.

And that told me everything.

I exhaled slowly. This was a setup.

A test? A joke? A prank? No idea.

I sighed, rubbing a hand down my face. "Alright, you guys? What's this about?"

Jisoo gave me a pointed look. "Guys?"

I rolled my eyes. "You know what that means. I am well aware you are Korean American and understand the context."

Jisoo snorted. "Oh, has someone been Googling me? Geez, Logan, if you wanted to get to know me better, you should have just asked."

Hye-won stretched luxuriously, arching her back like a cat. Her perfect stomach and legs were on display. "You seem tense. Something wrong, Captain?"

I looked at her deadpan.

Jisoo, who seemed a bit more reserved, let out a giggle, clearly playing along. "You saved our lives, Logan. It's not a big deal if you see a little skin, even by *accident*."

I closed my eyes for one full second.

Then I opened them, looking directly at Min-ji.

"Let me guess," I said dryly. "You got roped into this."

Min-ji swallowed hard, looking like she wanted to melt into the floor. "I—I tried to stop them."

I snorted. "Uh-huh."

She nodded furiously. "I did!"

That much, I actually believed.

Hye-won sighed dramatically. "Four ultra-hot, ultra-famous chicks are half-dressed in front of you, and this is how you react. Ugh. You're no fun."

I leveled her with a deeply unamused look.

"Did you really think this was going to work?" I asked, voice flat. "That I'd walk in here, take one look at the two of you playing femme fatale, and suddenly lose all sense of control?"

Jisoo shrugged, trying to look innocent. "No, but we thought you would at least take a picture."

I huffed a laugh, short and dry. "Do you want me to take a picture of you in a dressed-down state?"

Jisoo and Hye-won studied me. Hye-won spoke up. "And what if we said yes?"

"Then I will have to flick you in the forehead too."

I said it without thinking.

I turned to Ji-an. She was watching my reflection in the

mirror instead, completely still. Her eyes went wide when I said that. They then narrowed, and her cheeks went red.

Min-ji moved a bit from where she was standing. "Logan, who did you flick? And why?"

It was then that I let it out, laughing at how ridiculous the situation was.

"What about you, Ji-an?" I called out. "How do you feel about this situation?"

Surprisingly enough, she flipped me off as her face got redder.

It was adorable. Interesting.

I turned back to Hye-won and Jisoo, clapping my hands once. "Alright. I am properly awed by your incredible beauty. Show's over. Put some clothes on before someone walks in and accuses me of violating you or something."

Hye-won sighed but didn't argue.

Jisoo pouted.

Min-ji visibly relaxed.

And Ji-an?

She finally turned, walking past me like nothing happened, like she hadn't definitely been part of this, and muttered, "You're impossible."

I smirked. "And yet, here we are."

She didn't look at me again. Her face remained red.

I definitely won this round.

Hye-won was the last to move.

She stretched again, slow and lazy, clearly unbothered by the fact that she was standing in front of me in nothing but a bra and shorts.

I had already turned toward the door, fully prepared to leave this ridiculous situation behind, when she stepped into my path.

I stilled.

She smiled. "So, Captain."

I narrowed my eyes. "Hye-won."

She tilted her head, lips curling. "Since we're all feeling… grateful for your heroics, I was thinking."

I paused. Here we go.

She placed a hand on her hip, shifting her weight slightly. "How about a date?"

I blinked.

That… caught me off guard.

Not the flirtation—I expected that. Not the teasing—I expected that, too.

But a straight-up invitation?

That, I wasn't ready for.

I heard Min-ji choke on air.

Jisoo let out an amused little hum.

Ji-an, who had been walking away, stopped dead in her tracks.

Didn't turn around. Didn't move.

But I knew she was listening.

Hye-won was still watching me, completely at ease in her very minimal clothing, like she did this all the time. And honestly? She probably did.

I forced myself to blink, recovering. "A date."

She grinned. "Yeah. You. Me. Good food. Good drinks. No stalkers or murder attempts." She leaned in slightly, voice dropping. "You seem like a guy who could use a little fun, and I could definitely blow off some steam. And if you didn't know, in Nova, I am the sexy one."

I exhaled slowly, finally pulling my gaze away from her and rubbing a hand down my face.

"How would that even work? You leave in the morning."

She shrugged. "A little Netflix and chill."

I smirked, finally back in control. "You're unexpectedly straightforward."

She lifted a brow. "So, is that a yes?"

I almost laughed.

Hye-won was bold. I could respect that. But I also wasn't an idiot.

There were a thousand reasons I wasn't about to entertain this.

One, I was her security.

Two, this wasn't just any woman—it was one of the biggest K-pop idols on the planet. Trying to be casual with someone like that was a disaster waiting to happen.

Three?

There was a pair of very sharp eyes still locked onto my back, waiting for my response.

I glanced at Hye-won, expression unreadable. "I don't date clients."

She sighed dramatically. "Ugh. You're so boring."

I shrugged. "And yet, you asked."

She smirked. "Doesn't mean I'll stop trying."

Min-ji let out a small sound of horror.

Jisoo laughed.

And Ji-an?

She still hadn't moved.

Still hadn't turned around.

But for the first time since I walked in, her shoulders tensed.

I took that as my cue to get the hell out of here.

I looked at Hye-won one last time, smirking. "Good luck with that. You guys are wheels up in about fifty. Your CEO wants to go back to the hotel as soon as possible."

Then I turned, finally leaving the room.

And if I took one last glance at Ji-an before I left?

Well.

That was nobody's business but mine.

CHAPTER 33
JI-AN

"ARE YOU INSANE? WHY ON EARTH WOULD YOU ASK OUT Logan?" I rounded on Hye-won, still reeling from the audacity of it.

She just shrugged like it was the most obvious thing in the world. "He's tall, kind, witty, sexy as hell, and he saved our lives. Why wouldn't I ask him out?"

I blinked at her. "Don't you have a boyfriend?"

Hye-won flashed me a slow, smug smile. "Come on now, Ji-an. You know we don't do boyfriends. Besides, I'm not blind. I know you think he's cute. Actually, I'm well aware that you all think he's cute."

Jisoo giggled behind her hand, and Min-ji looked like she was seconds away from combusting.

I folded my arms. "Yes. He's attractive. Obviously. That's not the point. What were you going to do if he actually said yes?"

"Exactly what I said," Hye-won replied, completely

unfazed. "Take him back to my hotel room. Netflix and chill. I wonder if he likes sushi. I should ask him."

I narrowed my eyes. "You do actually know what that means, right?"

"Of course I do." She smirked. "Where do you think I got the vernacular?"

Then, with that same breezy, dangerous tone, she added, "I bet the boy's a beast in bed."

Jisoo burst out laughing, practically collapsing into a chair, while Min-ji mumbled something under her breath and covered her face.

I didn't even know what to say to that.

The thing about Hye-won is, you can never tell when she's joking. She's the flirtiest, the most teasing, the most outwardly confident of all of us—which is ironic, considering she comes from one of the most conservative political families in Korea. You'd never guess it watching her now.

She liked to have fun. That didn't make her scandalous. And honestly, to my knowledge, she'd only ever had two real boyfriends. So the implication that she'd take Logan to bed?

Probably just a joke.

Probably.

I shook my head. "Come on, ladies. We need to get ready to leave."

We started packing our things, slipping into sweatshirts and leggings as the stylists came in and roadies started clearing gear. The room buzzed with movement, makeup cases closing, outfits being stuffed into garment bags. Everyone had somewhere to be.

CHAPTER 34
LOGAN

THE VENUE HAD MOSTLY CLEARED OUT BY THE TIME I MADE MY way back toward the security wing. Most of the crew was packing up, the post-show adrenaline fading into exhaustion. It had been a successful night—no disturbances, no threats, no Brotherhood—and the girls had made it off stage without incident.

I'd call that a win.

Still, I wasn't ready to clock out just yet. There were final protocols to wrap up and a meeting to finish.

I knocked once, then pushed open the door to the private conference room set aside for post-show debriefs.

Inside, Mr. Lee was already seated at the head of the table, jacket off, shirt sleeves rolled up, speaking with someone on the phone in rapid Korean. At his right was Han Si-woo, leaning slightly back in his chair with one arm resting across his middle.

He was pale, tighter around the jaw than usual.

The stab wound he'd taken wasn't life-threatening, but it was bad enough to keep him from moving like himself. Still, he was dressed, presentable, and—because this was Han Si-woo—completely composed.

"Carter," Lee said as he ended the call. "Glad you're still here. Please, come in."

"Wouldn't miss it," I replied, stepping inside and closing the door behind me.

Min-hyuk was there, too, slouched in a chair like he had something better to do. Probably texting someone irrelevant about how annoyed he was to be stuck in a meeting with "the help."

I ignored him.

Lee stood and offered his hand. "Thank you. For everything."

I took it. "Just doing the job."

"No." His gaze sharpened. "You went beyond that. And I'm not the only one who noticed."

He reached into his inner coat pocket and pulled out an envelope—thick, sealed, and plainly not part of any company protocol.

"This isn't for Archangel," he said. "This is personal. You kept my girls safe when everything went to hell. That means more than you know."

I accepted the envelope without hesitation, slipping it into my vest. I'd argue about taking payment later.

"Much appreciated, sir."

Lee nodded, then glanced at Si-woo. "He's already been stitched up, but he's too stubborn to stay in bed."

Si-woo gave a small shrug. "Wasn't going to miss the debrief."

His voice was a little rougher than usual. Not weak, just edged with fatigue.

"I brought you something," he added, reaching behind the chair with his uninjured arm.

From beneath the table, he pulled out a sleek black gift bag and slid it across to me.

I opened it—and paused.

Inside was a boxed bottle of Hwayo X Premium 41, one of the rarest and most expensive soju labels in Korea. Smooth, high-proof, made from 100% rice, and aged in traditional earthenware. Probably a collector's bottle. Easily five hundred bucks, minimum.

"Damn," I said. "That's serious."

"It's from my father's cellar," Si-woo said simply. "I figured you'd appreciate something with a little bite."

"I do." I nodded. "Thanks. This is... incredible."

He gave me a tight smile. "You ever end up working in Seoul, give me a call. I've got a list of venues that actually give a damn about their security teams. Seoul Olympic Hall would kill to have someone like you on the ground. We've also been talking about the Wamu Theater in Seattle. Smaller, but high profile. Also a spot in Boise—Morrison Center. Bit off the radar, but decent size, big-name acts."

I raised an eyebrow. "You're scouting me already?"

"I'm practical," he said. "And I don't want amateurs around the girls again."

That landed. I could respect that.

He reached into his jacket and pulled out a slim black card, sliding it across the table. "That's my direct number. Don't hesitate."

I took the card, slipping it next to the envelope. "Thanks."

It was quiet for a moment—comfortable, professional.

Then Min-hyuk ruined it.

"You two done bro-hugging, or should we leave you alone with a bottle of wine and a sunset?"

Lee's expression barely changed, but his disappointment was loud.

Si-woo didn't even turn his head. "Try shutting up."

"I'm just saying," Min-hyuk went on, clearly enjoying himself. "We're bringing in real professionals tomorrow. Guys with actual credentials. Maybe Carter can go back to guarding parking lots."

I smiled slightly.

Lee stood, turning to his son. "You're excused."

"What?"

"I said, leave."

Min-hyuk scoffed, rolled his eyes, and muttered something under his breath as he stormed out, his shoes echoing across the tile.

The second the door clicked shut, Lee turned back to me. "Apologies. He's... not involved in anything that matters."

"Didn't take it personally," I said.

Lee nodded. "Good. Then let's finish up the last details."

And we did.

We went over the full timeline, the exits, the morning transport schedule, and the addition of private contractors at the hotel. Everything had been accounted for. Every scenario.

And by the end of it, I had one clear objective in mind.

Make sure this chapter ended clean.

Because something told me this wasn't the end.

Not by a long shot.

I stepped out of the main admin building with Mr. Lee and Si-woo, the night air hitting me like a sigh I hadn't realized I'd been holding. Most of Nova's crew had already packed up. Gear cases were loaded, cables coiled, tents broken down. The venue was emptying fast, swallowed by the dark stretch of the Columbia Gorge.

Si-woo limped slightly as one of his men helped him toward their transport, his usual precision dulled by the pain he pretended not to feel. Mr. Lee slid into the back of a matte black SUV, his son trailing behind him like a sullen shadow, muttering something under his breath. One of the junior stylists laughed too loudly, her voice vanishing into the distance as she disappeared around the far side of the lot.

That should've been it.

But someone was still here.

I turned—and saw Ji-an.

She wasn't talking. Wasn't moving.

She was just… watching me.

The overhead lights painted long shadows across the

parking lot, and for a second, I thought she might just wave goodbye and leave it at that.

But she didn't.

Instead, she walked right up to me—head high, shoulders squared, her movements deliberate. She looked more like the woman I'd seen on stage earlier, all grace and power... but with something else simmering beneath the surface.

When she reached me, she didn't say anything. Just looked up at me for a heartbeat too long. Then, without a word, she grabbed my hand.

I didn't resist.

She tugged gently, leading me behind one of the massive transport trucks parked near the edge of the lot—out of sight, out of earshot. The roar of the river was louder here, the wind carrying the scent of sage and dust and maybe a hint of rain. The hum of the stage crew, the chatter of staff, the shuffle of closing time—all of it fell away.

And for a moment, it felt like we were the only two people in the world.

Ji-an stopped walking. Turned to face me. She released my hand.

The moonlight caught in her hair. Her lips parted slightly, but she didn't speak.

I kept my hands in my pockets, trying not to think about how close she was. Trying not to think about how good she looked in that oversized hoodie, makeup off, eyes bright.

"You know," she said softly, "I probably won't see you again."

I glanced at her. "Not unless you play here again. I was hired for this venue. That job's done."

She nodded, lips pressing together. "Right."

A long pause. Then, "So that's it?"

I looked at her again, really looked at her. "Was there something else?"

She glared. "You're not going to ask for my contact information, phone number, nothing?"

"I hadn't planned on it."

"Why?"

I cocked an eyebrow. "You seem to have a knack for pulling me into uncomfortable conversations."

She put a piece of paper in my hand. "My personal cell. If you don't text me, I am going to announce on social media that you are my boyfriend and you've asked me to marry you."

I gawked at her. "You do realize that will do more damage to your reputation than mine, right?"

"Maybe," she shrugged. "But it will annoy you, and I know how you hate to be annoyed."

I snorted. "This seems totally unnecessary."

She smiled, and her face lit up the night. "Logan."

"Yeah?"

"One more thing."

And then—

She reached up.

Her fingers curled into the collar of my jacket, light at first, then firmer. She stepped in again, close enough now that I could feel her breath against my throat.

"I told myself I wouldn't," she murmured, almost like she was talking to herself. "Told myself you're too calm. Too rational. Too different. Too... American."

I raised an eyebrow. "Those are your deal-breakers?"

She smiled. Just barely. "Apparently not."

And then she kissed me.

Not a brush. Not an accident.

She kissed me with reckless abandon.

Her mouth met mine with a rush of heat that hit me straight in the chest. I didn't move at first—maybe out of surprise, maybe because if I did move, I wouldn't stop. But then her hand slid up into my hair, fingers curling at the base of my neck, and my body betrayed me.

And lord help me. I kissed her back.

One hand slipped to her waist, then higher, finding the curve of her back. I pulled her in just enough to feel her against me, solid and real and infuriatingly perfect. She made a small sound—half sigh, half gasp—and I swallowed it like it was oxygen.

And then just as quickly, she pulled back.

Her breathing was uneven. Her lips were slightly parted. Her fingers were still fisted in my jacket.

"Yeah," she said, voice quiet and rough, "I bet you regret flicking me now."

I smiled in spite of myself. "Ji-an, I—"

She stepped back, just a fraction, and put a hand up, cutting me off.

"No speeches. No questions, no awkward pauses," she

whispered. "In fact, shut up. Not another word. Thank you for saving my life and the lives of my friends."

Then she turned toward the waiting cars.

I stood there, heart thudding harder than it had all night, watching the woman who had just turned my entire sense of control into dust walk away without looking back.

And for the first time in a very long time—

I didn't know what the hell to do next.

CHAPTER 35
JI-AN

I DIDN'T SAY GOODBYE.

I didn't look back.

I just walked to the bus like I hadn't just kissed the man who had been living rent-free in my head for nearly a year. Like I hadn't just grabbed Logan Carter by the jacket and kissed him with the kind of desperate intensity that I had only seen in movies.

But this had been me. And my actions had been real. *Too real.*

And now?

Now I was absolutely, completely, and *utterly* screwed.

Next to me, my friends and bandmates asked questions. I answered—we probably had an entire conversation.

But sitting in the dark of the tour bus, the hum of the road beneath us,

I can't remember a single word I said.

I realized too late that I was panicking.

Full-body, heart-racing, stomach-swooping panicking.

Not because I regretted it.

No. That would've been easier.

I was panicking because it was so good.

Because the second his mouth touched mine, something in me snapped.

And worse?

Something in him answered.

I felt it.

The way his hands moved. The way he pulled me just close enough. The way he kissed me back like he'd been trying not to for days, maybe weeks, maybe months.

Like I wasn't Ji-an of Nova.

Like I was just me.

Just Ji-an.

I swallowed hard, staring out the window as the car pulled away from the venue. The Gorge disappeared behind us in the mirror, the stage lights a glowing blur in the distance.

He didn't chase me.

Not that I thought he would. Not that I wanted him to.

I mean, I did. But also—no. But also—yes, I did.

This was ridiculous.

I was ridiculous.

And the worst part?

I was leaving.

Right now I am on a bus. To another venue. Then a car to a different place. Then a private plane. Seoul, Tokyo, Jakarta, Bangkok. Another leg of the tour. Another set of hotel rooms.

Another wave of cameras and interviews and curated, professional, untouchable Ji-an.

And Logan Carter?

He'd still be here.

Back to private security. Back to whatever job came next. Back to a life that didn't have room for girls like me.

He wasn't coming with us.

I hadn't asked him to.

I couldn't.

Because I didn't even know what this was.

A kiss? A thank you? A declaration of love? A disaster?

I pressed the heels of my hands to my eyes and leaned back in the seat, breathing deep. I could feel Min-ji watching me. Feel the way Jisoo kept glancing at me in the mirror. Hye-won was practically vibrating.

But for once, no one said anything else.

Maybe because they knew.

Maybe because, for the first time, they saw it.

That I wasn't just being dramatic.

That I wasn't just curious or flirty or letting a crush get the best of me.

That I had feelings for him.

Real ones.

And now I had to leave him behind.

And the stupid, selfish, terrifying truth?

I didn't want to.

CHAPTER 36
HYE-WON

THE BUS RIDE WAS QUIET.

Too quiet.

Ji-an was in the front, earphones in, forehead pressed against the tinted glass like we couldn't all tell she was spiraling. Min-ji sat stiff as a rod next to her, watching her like a worried cat. Jisoo was flipping through TikTok, trying and failing to act like the air wasn't thick with tension.

And me?

I was lounging in the back, one leg kicked up over the other, flipping through my camera roll.

Because I knew something they didn't.

I knew exactly who Logan Carter was.

I'd recognized him the second he stepped into that security office on day one, all stoic eyes and forearms and no-nonsense everything. But it hadn't clicked until just after the show. Not until I scrolled back through old photos from last year—Hong Kong airport. Ji-an, all dressed down in a hoodie and baseball cap, talking to some hot stranger for almost an hour.

I'd taken a photo of it. A joke, back then. Something to tease her about later.

But the guy?

It was him.

Same jawline. Same eyes. Same swagger. Same vibe. Logan Carter.

Ji-an had known him.

And she'd said nothing.

I stared at the photo again, zooming in. Her expression in that picture was soft. Curious. Vulnerable.

Then I swiped to the next one.

This one was recent. The video. The one I'd pulled from our internal security team's shared drive before it could be scrubbed clean. Logan bursting out of the dark like a damn superhero. One bullet. Five men on the ground. That last guy's face when Logan dropped him like a sack of rice? Iconic.

I watched it again.

Bit my lip.

The truth was—I liked him.

Not the slow, shy, rom-com kind of like. I wasn't that girl. Never had been.

But Logan? Logan was my type. Big. Military. Unshakeable. The kind of man who didn't flinch when things got messy. The kind of man who made you feel safe just by being near him. I liked that.

And I wanted him.

The problem was... so did Ji-an.

And honestly? That made it more fun.

She was too careful. Too closed off. Always trying to control the narrative, even around us. But the second she stepped off that bus earlier, cheeks flushed, lips parted, looking like she just barely survived a category-five emotional hurricane—I knew she kissed him.

And I was willing to guess; she hadn't been the only one affected.

So here I was. Back of the bus. Everyone pretending nothing had happened.

And me? Ready to break the internet.

I opened my mail app, typed in a burner email I used when I was bored and feeling petty, and started composing a message.

TO: PRESS@KSTARWATCHER.COM
SUBJECT: NOVA SECURITY SCANDAL?
BODY:
YOU DIDN'T HEAR IT FROM ME. BUT IF
YOU'RE WONDERING WHY THE BUZZ
AROUND NOVA'S LATEST CONCERT IS
SPIKING, MAYBE CHECK THE
ATTACHED FOOTAGE. SEEMS LIKE
SOMEONE FORGOT TO MENTION A
HEROIC SECURITY GUARD—OR THE
FACT THAT HE'S VERY CLOSE TO THE
MEMBERS OF NOVA.
ATTACHMENT: THE GORGE
INCIDENT.MOV

I hovered my finger over the send button. Just for a second.

Because yeah, it was chaos.

But it was fun chaos.

I hit send.

Closed the app.

Leaned back and smiled to myself as Ji-an glanced over her shoulder, her brows pinched like she could feel the storm coming.

Oh, baby.

You have no idea.

ABOUT THE AUTHOR

Marlee Earl writes swoon-worthy stories with heat, heart, and high-stakes emotion. Known for crafting unforgettable characters and electric chemistry, she explores the messy, passionate corners of fame, romance, and identity. *Fanservice* is her debut in the romantic drama space—but not her first time telling a story that sticks with you long after the last page.

When she's not writing, Marlee is wrangling kids, bingeing K-dramas, or plotting her next book from a coffee shop corner.

Follow Marlee and get bonus content at **Silverstone-Books.com**.

J.C. Anderson

Pen name of Collin Earl

J.C. Anderson is the darker, grittier pen name of best-selling author **Collin Earl**—used for stories that bend genre boundaries and explore complex characters in morally gray worlds. Whether it's suspense-laced romance, psychological twists, or speculative fiction with an edge, J.C. Anderson brings a bold voice to stories that aren't afraid to get messy.

To learn more and explore other works, visit **Silverstone-Books.com**.

www.ingramcontent.com/pod-product-compliance
Lightning Source LLC
Chambersburg PA
CBHW031944010726
47493CB00007B/2076